# Darkbeast

Also by Morgan Keyes

*Darkbeast Rebellion*

# Darkbeast

## MORGAN KEYES

*Morgan Keyes*

*Margaret K. McElderry Books*

NEW YORK   LONDON   TORONTO   SYDNEY   NEW DELHI

MARGARET K. McELDERRY BOOKS
An imprint of Simon & Schuster Children's Publishing Division
1230 Avenue of the Americas, New York, New York 10020

This book is a work of fiction. Any references to historical events, real people, or real places are used fictitiously. Other names, characters, places, and events are products of the author's imagination, and any resemblance to actual events or places or persons, living or dead, is entirely coincidental.

MARGARET K. MCELDERRY BOOKS is a trademark of Simon & Schuster, Inc.

For information about special discounts for bulk purchases, please contact Simon & Schuster Special Sales at 1-866-506-1949 or business@simonandschuster.com.

The Simon & Schuster Speakers Bureau can bring authors to your live event. For more information or to book an event, contact the Simon & Schuster Speakers Bureau at 1-866-248-3049 or visit our website at www.simonspeakers.com.

Also available in a Margaret K. McElderry Books hardcover edition

Interior design by Mike Rosamilia

Cover design by Russell Gordon

The text for this book is set in Adobe Caslon Pro.

Manufactured in the United States of America

0215 OFF

First Margaret K. McElderry Books paperback edition September 2013

2 4 6 8 10 9 7 5 3

The Library of Congress has cataloged the hardcover edition as follows:

Keyes, Morgan.

Darkbeast / Morgan Keyes.—1st ed.

p. cm.

Summary: Twelve-year-old Keara runs away rather than sacrifice Caw, the darkbeast she has been bound to all her life, and, pursued by the Inquisitors who would punish her for heresy, she joins a performing troupe of Travelers.

ISBN 978-1-4424-4205-4 (hardcover)

ISBN 978-1-4424-4207-8 (eBook)

[1. Fantasy.] I. Title.

PZ7.K52614Dar 2012

[Fic]—dc23

2011040301

ISBN 978-1-4424-4206-1 (pbk)

*To Mom and Dad,*
*who set me on my own Great Road when*
*they first introduced me to books*

# ACKNOWLEDGMENTS

Books like *Darkbeast* would never exist without the help of many people.

I am especially grateful to Julie Czerneda, the editor who chose to publish the short story where Caw first appeared. Also, I am indebted to my agent, Richard Curtis, who read that story and refused to let Caw sleep. My First Reader, Bruce Sundrud, was key to my getting this book right.

I have been overwhelmed by the incredible folks at Simon & Schuster Children's Publishing—Karen Wojtyla and Emily Fabre and all the other hard-working souls who have been responsible for placing this book in your hands.

Throughout my writing, I have been buoyed by my very own "troupe," my family members—Klaskys, Fallons, Maddreys, and Timminses—who are always willing to lend their enthusiasm to my ventures. Mark Maddrey deserves very special thanks for his constant, unwavering support of me and my writing career.

Of course, no revel is complete without an audience—the readers of this book. I hope you will stop by my website: morgankeyes.com.

# PART ONE

# Rebellion

# Chapter One

The Travelers arrived in Silver Hollow a week before my twelfth nameday.

We heard about them long before their wagons rolled onto our village green. Rumors swept over the plains, moving faster than the summer breeze that flattened the gray-green grass. My oldest sister first told me that the Travelers were drawing near. She had heard about them from her husband, who had spoken to the miller in the next village, who had listened to the bargemen who plied the river all the way to the Primate's home in the far-off city of Lutecia, capital of all Duodecia.

I dreamed about the Travelers every night. I had memorized all their magical tales about the days when the gods still walked the earth. But once the Travelers' wagons filled the green, Mother forbade me to see them.

"Keara," she said in the voice she used when every bone in her body was weary to the point of breaking. "You are too young to understand their stories."

"I'm not too young! I already know their stories. Besides, I'm almost a woman—I'll be twelve next week!"

"Just because you can memorize words does not mean that you understand the thought behind them. And moving into the Women's Hall does not automatically teach you all the lessons the world has to offer, either. You can see the Travelers the next time they come to Silver Hollow."

"But they haven't been here in eight years! I'll be *ancient* before they come back. I'll be old and boring and married!"

"Then you can stand beside your husband, and you'll both enjoy the Travelers together. If any man ever weds a girl as stubborn as you, Keara."

I knew the real reason that Mother wanted me to stay inside our one-room cottage. She feared the Primate's titheman. He was due in the village any day, and the tattooed band around my wrist had faded to almost nothing. The careful violet knot, now almost two years old, was nearly invisible beneath dirt and my sun-darkened summer skin.

Mother had missed paying my head tax the year before. She

had been short on coins, and I had been forced to hide in our cottage for the entire three days that the titheman stayed on the green. None of the villagers had given me up, though, thank all the gods.

Of course, there was no way to avoid paying the head tax this year. I would never be allowed in Bestius's godhouse on my name-day if I didn't have a fresh tattoo. But every day of savings counted when copper coins weighed in the balance. Every day counted when the ewes had thrown only singletons in the spring, not a twin to be found anywhere on the plains. Every day counted when a widow was raising a headstrong daughter, alone and unaided.

Tithe tattoo or no, I sneaked out of the cottage and watched the first night of the Travelers' plays. I wasn't a fool. I waited until Mother had left, until she had bustled off to meet my middle sister, Morva, in the Women's Hall. They were going to watch the Travelers together. Alone in our home, I tugged on my finest clothes, Morva's old gown that Mother had cut down for me to wear on the goddess Pondera's gloryday that past spring. I slipped my feet into Mother's prize sandals, the ones with the fake jewels woven around the ankles.

Mindful that I mustn't be seen, I lurked at the back of the crowd. That meant I missed a few of the lines, lost the words in the rustle of the people around me.

But I could see the Travelers' costumes. I tried to imagine

how anyone could weave an entire cloak from gold. My fingers clenched as if I were the one gathering up the pleats of a sweeping velvet skirt. I could make out every shimmering stitch on the brilliant masks, and I gaped at the richly embroidered shapes that transformed ordinary men and women into gods and goddesses, into the Twelve.

The Travelers spoke to me with a magic stronger than anything Mother had ever brewed from her stash of common herbs. They were even more compelling than my bond with my darkbeast. Inside my mind the Travelers were the most beautiful sunset I had ever seen, the finest feast I had ever eaten, the deepest emotion I had ever felt, all rolled into one rollicking, painted caravan.

I started trembling from the very first word. An old man introduced the troupe, announcing that they were going to perform *Patrius and the First Primate*. The speaker's voice was loud enough to shake the wooden columns on Pondera's godhouse, all the way at the southern edge of the village. His face was carved with deep lines, and the skin on his hands looked like parchment, even in the flickering torchlight. His beard curled like a lamb's pelt, swirling in and out of the massive iron necklace that covered half his chest.

His eyes found me where I lurked in the shadows. They read me, all the way down to the marrow of my bones. The Traveler could have been speaking only to me, only *for* me.

I shivered as hard as when I had blackwater fever, two summers before. The air around me was hot—we were almost to the Thunder Moon, after all—but gooseflesh rose on my arms. The old man stepped behind a curtain, and another man appeared, the Traveler playing Patrius. His words thundered over the crowd, echoing with the power and majesty and greatness of the father of all the gods.

A third man played First Primate Kerwen, the ancient leader of Duodecia. Kerwen was a brave warrior. He fought battle after battle, but he could never best the tribes around him. One night, after a terrible raid, Kerwen vowed fealty to any who would aid him in his battle against the other tribes.

Patrius came to him then, demanding that Kerwen humble himself. Kerwen knelt for twelve days in the freezing flow of the Silver River, without food, without rest, without succor. Only then did Patrius make Kerwen the Primate, the ruler over all the people of Duodecia. Patrius vowed that Kerwen's sons would reign as long as they stayed loyal to the Twelve, as long as they bent their knee to all the gods and goddesses who walked the realm. After Kerwen affirmed his devotion to the Twelve, and to Patrius most of all, the gods became stars and strode into the sky.

As the play drew to a close, a white stag blazed out against the velvet curtain at the back of the Travelers' stage. It was as bright as silver, but it burned with some cold flame that did not consume the stage. The stag was Patrius's sign, a reminder of all the power that the father of the gods had shared with First Primate Kerwen, of all the glory still held by the royal house so many generations later.

As the glow slowly faded, a complementary excitement blazed up inside me. The Travelers took their bows, and I wriggled into the very front row of spectators, clapping hard enough that my palms stung. Sweat made my auburn hair curl against my neck. There was hardly a breeze on that summer night, but I did not care. I did not care about anything more than honoring the Travelers.

Of course Mother saw me as soon as I left the safety of the shadows. She dragged me home by my ear, ignoring my outraged squawks, and she leashed me to Caw's cage. That was the first time she'd bound me in over a year. I started to protest, but she only hissed, "Take it to your darkbeast!"

*"Good evening,"* Caw said as soon as Mother stormed out of the cottage. I knew that she was heading over to my oldest sister's tiny home. Mother and Robina would talk about me—about my failings, about my disobedience—long into the night. Caw's bright eyes sparkled as he asked, *"Treats?"*

I shrugged and reached into the pottery jar on the mantel, digging out a few chunks of dried apple. There was no crisis so great that Caw would not beg for treats. He gulped down every bite before thinking a reluctant, *"Thank you."* I knew that tone of voice. I knew he hoped for more.

I could hear Caw's familiar speech inside my head. We had been bound to each other ever since I was an infant. Mother had presented me to Bestius on the night of the Thunder Moon, the first full moon after my birth. I could not count how many times Mother had told me about how the god of all darkbeasts had sent Caw just for me, finding me on the bare onyx altar in Bestius's godhouse.

Mother often recited how she had given me my name, announcing to Bestius and all the other gods that I would be called Keara. Then Caw had swooped down to the altar, displaying his jet-black wings as he cocked his head to examine me. I had laughed at his funny, scratchy voice. Me—a twelve-day-old child—already laughing! The priest, come all the way from Rivermeet, had wasted no time speaking his strongest prayer to bind the raven to me. Mother had sealed the bond with her most valuable herbs, blowing a dusty mixture of sweet ladysilk and bitter mudroyal into my nose, into Caw's. My darkbeast and I had sneezed at the same time.

Ever since, Caw's words had resonated deep inside me. When I had something to say to him, though, I almost always spoke out loud. That was an old habit, one I had never tried to break, not through all the long hours we'd spent together. Caw and I often wandered far from Silver Hollow, ranging as far as the hills when we gathered berries and windfall apples, or collected the herbs that Mother dried and sold in distant Rivermeet. It never seemed important to think to Caw silently, the way so many other children did to their own darkbeasts.

Of course, Caw was different from all those other animals. He wasn't disgusting, like the rats and snakes that took the evil thoughts of other children. He wasn't angry or sly or dirty. He was my darkbeast, and he was perfect for me.

I stepped toward his cage, and my jeweled sandal caught on the rough dirt floor. I fell hard, skinning my knee through the fine fabric of Morva's dress. My bare palms scraped on the ground, and I scarcely remembered not to use the words I'd heard the shepherds say when they thought they were alone with their flocks. I could hear Mother's sternest voice all over again: "Take it to your darkbeast."

Caw turned his head to the side as I used my fabric leash to dab at my bleeding palm. *I heard applause coming from the green. It sounds as if the Travelers put on quite a performance.*

"They were wonderful," I whispered, already forgetting my stinging flesh as I remembered the amazing play. "I've never seen anything like them."

*You were wrong to disobey your mother, Keara-ti. She only thought to protect you.*

I ignored the endearment that Caw attached to my name, the ending that was only suitable for a child. I let my annoyance with

Mother sharpen my tone. "Protect me from what? She just doesn't want to pay the titheman!"

*"There are more dangers in the world than handing over the Primate's head tax."*

"There's nothing dangerous about watching Travelers in my own village, standing on my own village green!"

*"The danger is in your growing up. Your leaving her behind. The danger is that you will no longer be a child."*

I scoffed. "Mother can't wait for me to be out of this cottage. She can't wait to have all the blankets to herself, to brew her nasty whiteroot tea without making something else for me."

*"Your mother dreads the day you leave her. You're her last child. Her baby."*

"I'm not a baby!" I could not keep a whine out of my voice as I complained to Caw. "I'm nearly a woman, Caw. Nearly a woman, and Mother still said I wouldn't understand the plays. She was wrong, though. I understood every word."

*"Every word?"*

I thought about the Travelers' story. In the revel Kerwen had mourned a lost wife, murdered children. He had wept with a husband's grief, with a parent's devastation.

Well, of course I could not understand *that*. Not completely. My own mother would never grieve for me. She had a heart of stone. "I understood nearly every word," I said defensively.

*"You don't have much longer to live beneath your mother's roof. Be kind to her while you can."*

How could I be kind to someone who was so cruel to me? So strict? Who bound me closer to her than I had ever been bound to Caw's iron cage? I closed my fingers around those cold bars and said, "I cannot wait for the day that I'm free to live in the Women's Hall."

Caw shifted in his cage, ruffling his feathers as he resettled on his perch. The motion was enough to remind me that my nameday was not the best thing that would ever happen to me—even though it would mean getting out of the cottage that I shared with Mother. Certainly, my nameday would bring me freedom. But that freedom came at a cost, a price I was still not certain I could pay. "I'm sorry," I said after a long moment. "I didn't mean that. I just wish that I was free! You wouldn't understand."

*"No,"* Caw said, and his voice was dry inside my head. *"I cannot imagine how* freedom *would feel."*

I looked at the leash that bound my wrist, the old rags that I could slip off anytime I chose. My fingers curled around the iron bars of Caw's cage. "I'm sorry," I said again, and I truly was contrite. "I should think more carefully before I speak." Caw didn't reply, and I knew that he was waiting for me to say more, to make another admission. I sighed and dug my toe into the earthen floor. "I was wrong. I should not have defied Mother."

Caw peered at me through the bars of his cage, tilting his

head at a familiar angle. *"I take your rebellion,"* he said. *"Forget it. It is mine."*

Immediately I felt the familiar sensation of lightness, as if I were floating like a tuft of thistledown on a spring breeze. The roof of my mouth tingled. My breath caught and trembled inside my body, like a thousand butterfly wings brushing beneath my skin.

I turned my face toward the ceiling. I spread my arms by my sides. I pushed my tongue against the back of my teeth, determined to make the sensation last as long as possible.

I could not imagine never again feeling this way. I could not imagine never again hearing my darkbeast's voice, never again listening to his well-worn formula. I could not imagine what my life would be like after I became a proper woman among my people on my twelfth nameday. After I had sacrificed Caw on the cool onyx altar in the center of Bestius's godhouse.

# Chapter Two

The following morning I woke as the sun rose. Caw was watching me from his cage, his sharp eyes glinting in the early-morning light. I eased him from his perch, letting him dig his claws into the special padding that I wore on my left shoulder.

*"Treats?"* he asked, as I walked by the fireplace.

"Work first." Caw ruffled his feathers in obvious disappointment, but Mother looked up from the bread she was making. She nodded once—a thin measure of approval, even if she hadn't actually heard Caw's plaintive request.

Well, thin was better than nothing. Better than I deserved, for having sneaked out to see the Travelers. I hurried outside to free the chickens from the coop, where they had safely spent the night.

The Travelers ... Once again I thought about the play I had watched—the power of the actors' voices, the beauty of their costumes. If I concentrated hard enough, I could recall the rhythm of their lines. Not all the words, of course, but a snatch of rhyme here and there.

*"Fool!"* Caw's voice was sharp inside my head. I started to protest, but I quickly realized that he was looking down on a chicken. One of the silly hens was pecking my shoes, as if the worn leather would fill her belly.

"Not all birds can be brilliant like you," I said. I spread food scraps in a wide circle so that the chickens would not fight. Caw grumbled as he maintained his perch, easily parsing the sarcasm in my tone.

Without prompting from Mother, I dragged two empty buckets to the well and filled them with water. I took care not to spill any as I carried the heavy load back to our cottage. As I began to collect eggs from the coop, I said to Caw, "I still feel bad about sneaking out last night. Does that mean I'm becoming more mature?"

*"Hardly,"* he said, and his voice was dry. *"It means you're hoping to be forgiven. You're hoping for permission to see the Travelers tonight."*

"Caw!" I protested. But he was right. A part of me wanted Mother to reward me for my diligence. Maybe I could sort some seeds for her. Grind some dried herbs for poultices.

*"Perhaps they'll perform* Bestius and the Darkbeasts.*"*

I tried to imagine the Travelers' play. There would be a gathering of all the darkbeasts, of creatures specially bred by Bestius's priests. The holy man would choose the best animal for the newborn on his altar. There would be prayers, and sacred oil traced over the child's head and hands and belly, and then the words of Binding.

I tried to imagine how the Travelers would show the moment of transformation, the instant that the darkbeast was irrevocably tied to its child. Music could never be enough. Costumes could not explain. Even the finest rhymes would fall flat.

"Do you remember, Caw? The day that we were bound?"

*"Of course I remember,"* my darkbeast said. *"I remember everything."* There was pride in his voice. No one took pride from darkbeasts. No one took any of their flaws.

"What was it like?"

*"It was hot inside the godhouse. The altar was ringed with a dozen candles, the tall ones, as thick as your arm. And it was noisy, too. You would not stop screeching."*

"I must have been scared!"

*"Or hungry. I was hungry. No one fed me for* days *before the Bonding."*

Caw was eyeing the eggs in my basket a little too fondly. "Days or hours," I said. "It's all the same to you."

I shooed him through the door in front of me, watching him flutter back inside his cage. He settled onto his perch gingerly, as if he barely had the strength to balance. I rolled my eyes, but I gave him the heel of bread Mother had left drying on the table. "Here, you monster," I said.

*"That's all? Just one bite of bread?"*

"That's enough for a grown man to break his fast!" Nevertheless, I added a handful of dried apple treats.

Mother nodded with approval as she counted the eggs. Each hen had laid during the night. "I'll make you a seedcake this afternoon, Keara-ti," she said. As she said the diminutive form of my name, I realized I was truly forgiven for sneaking out.

I was forgiven, and Caw was right. Mother's talk of danger, of forbidding me to see the Travelers, was not actually about anything evil lurking on the green. Mother truly liked keeping me close to her, living in her house, sharing in her life, and she did not want that time to end. The thought was so astonishing that I nearly dropped the clay pot of apple treats.

Before I could pursue the notion further, Mother said, "But now let us pay the titheman."

"The titheman!"

How could Mother possibly know that the Primate's man had arrived in our village? Someone must have told her while I was collecting water from the well. The news would travel fast through

Silver Hollow. Anyone who could not afford the head tax would be forced to hide—as I had, the year before.

As I watched, Mother reached beneath our mattress, wriggling her wise fingers into the careful slit in the very middle of the underside. I knew that the leather pouch she extracted smelled of lavender and fresh grass; I had handled it a dozen times before. Mother loosed the ties carefully, as if she feared spilling the contents across our earthen floor.

One by one she counted out her coins—bright copper disks that glowed as if they'd captured all the light of the sun. Twelve in all—one for each year that I had already lived, plus one for the year to come.

I watched eagerly. The titheman would demand double payment, last year as well as this, and a full copper in penalty for my missing the counting the last time he had come to Silver Hollow.

If Mother did not count out the second set of twelve coins, I would be responsible for the payment. Many parents did not pay for their children the year that they became adults. We children could borrow from Aurelius's godhouse, from the donations made to the god of wealth. It was a challenge to start our first years as adults deep in debt, but many of us—most of us—had little choice.

Mother finished stacking her twelve coins into a precious tower. She ticked her ridged fingernail down the column, double-checking her counting. When she was certain, she scooped the coppers into her worn woolen pouch, hiding the money away in the folds of her skirt.

There. Mother was going to pay for only one year. I was responsible for the other on my own.

I folded my hands into fists, keeping them out of Mother's sight. She was absolutely within her rights. No parent owed a child the final head tax. Besides, it was good training, for every year of the rest of my life. I glanced at Caw, hoping he was watching me, that he saw how mature I was being. My darkbeast, though, had fallen asleep after gulping down his food. His head was hunched toward his chest.

Mother led the way out the door, through the village, down to the green, where our neighbors' milk cows grazed among the Travelers' brightly painted wagons. The titheman had set up his table beneath the oak tree on the far end of the grassy swath, away from the chaos of the performers. This was the same man who had come to us two years before. He was old, with gray hair that looked as light as summer fog. His heavy jowls pulled his lips into a permanent frown, melting his face like a tallow candle left too close to the fire.

His iron cask hulked at his feet, squat and ugly. I wondered how much it weighed, if I could possibly lift it. Not that I would ever get the chance—not with the two massive guards who stood on either side of the titheman. Only a fool would think of fighting them for the cask, for the coins collected from every corner of Duodecia. The soldiers' arms were as big around as my waist. Legend said that each member of the Primate's Guard carried a dozen different weapons, most of them hidden until they were called into deadly use. Nevertheless, their swords were in plain sight—long and sharp and lethal.

I swallowed hard and hung back, letting Mother speak her case. She made short work of paying her own tithe, handing over a single precious silver and receiving a fresh tattoo around her own wrist. Without the Primate's mark, she would never be allowed to sell her herbs in the market at Rivermeet. I tried not to be jealous that she paid for herself instead of paying for me in the coming year.

Once her own business was done, Mother dug deep in her skirts and rescued the woolen pouch she had shown me in the cottage. She extracted her coins one by one, counting them out as if they were gold instead of copper. When the twelve disks rested on the titheman's table, Mother recited the traditional words: "I present my daughter Keara, who desires to be counted among all the loyal subjects of the Primate. Long live Primate Hendor!"

The titheman completed the formula. "Long live Primate Hendor." His voice was dry and crumbly and bored. Almost as an afterthought, he reached for his scroll of office, holding it aloft, as he was required to do. "Let . . . Keara of Silver Dale step forward and be counted as one of the Primate's loyal—"

"Hollow," I said, interrupting the titheman. He frowned at me, his long face dripping even lower. Mother stiffened, but she did not gainsay me. "This village is Silver *Hollow*. I am Keara of Silver Hollow."

The titheman harrumphed and glanced down at his scroll. "Hollow," he acknowledged. I wondered where Silver Dale was, and if there was a girl there named Keara. "Keara of Silver Hollow."

He dipped an enormous plumed pen into an inkwell and started to scratch on his scroll. The nib must have been newly sharpened; I could hear it cut deep into the parchment as it shed its ink. I could not imagine what the titheman was writing—he added word after word, never once looking up at Mother or me.

I considered clearing my throat to remind him that we were waiting, but I knew Mother would never approve. Instead I made myself stand perfectly still. I pretended that I was a Traveler, that I was performing some role in a play. Which of the gods would keep a human girl waiting for an eternity?

Who was I fooling? Any of them would.

The titheman read over his handiwork, his lips moving as he eyed each word. Finally he pushed himself back from his table and glared at me down his nose. "There are twelve coins here. But the Primate's records indicate a missed year. These twelve coins will count for eleven and a penalty. But where is the head tax for the coming year? I'll not paint the tithe tattoo unless you clear all your debt."

Mother looked at me. I looked back at her. I think we both had hoped that the titheman wouldn't notice, that his records would be incomplete.

At last I shrugged and stepped back, ready to head to Aurelius's godhouse. I could borrow the tithe and be back before the ink dried on the old man's scroll. If only the paying back would prove so easy.

"Blessed be Aurelius," I muttered, "who aids all those in need."

The titheman's lips pursed, as if he had sucked on a blade of bitterroot. "Blessed be Aurelius. Be quick, then. There are others waiting."

I looked around the green. No one else was waiting, not so early in the morning. I bit off my reply, though, substituting a polite "Thank you, lord," for all the things I wanted to say.

Mother let me take three steps away before she called my name. When I turned back, there was a smile on her lips. "Why, what is this?" She pulled another pouch from her skirts. I recognized it as the knit bag I had made for her years before, for one of Madrina's glorydays long past. The stitches were rough—the uneven work of a child new to knitting needles. I'd had no idea that Mother still owned the thing. I was so surprised I could only give her a questioning look.

For answer she shook the bag, and I heard the jangle of metal against metal. Hope fluttered in my throat like a new-hatched chick, and I moved back to stand with the adults.

"Mother?" I asked, folding a dozen possibilities into the word.

She turned back to the titheman and started to count out more copper. Twelve coins, each brighter than the one before. I could only guess how many bundles of herbs Mother must have sold at the Rivermeet market, how successful she had been without my ever knowing, to have so many extra coins at her disposal. "There," she said to the titheman. "That should clear the debt."

Once again the titheman scrutinized the coins, as if he believed Mother would cheat him, but I knew that was impossible. Mother never lied. She'd given that vice to her darkbeast decades before, and I was certain she had never been tempted to stray back into evil.

"Twelve," the titheman said at last. He scratched something new onto his scroll, something that he underlined three times. He barely looked at me as he intoned, "Let Keara be counted among the Primate's loyal children. Let Keara be protected by all the Primate's power."

I longed to say something to Mother. I wanted to thank her, to tell her how much I appreciated her payment. Now I could start my first year as a woman clear and free from debt. I wouldn't be forced to scramble and scrounge, to beg jobs from our neighbors. I was grateful. But even more than that, I was touched. Caw had been right. Mother *did* love me—even when she made me think that she didn't care, that I was only a cause for bitter disappointment.

I stayed silent, though. The titheman's grim presence stilled my tongue, him and his massive guards. Wordless, I watched the sour-faced old man curl his scroll and wrap it with a velvet ribbon. One of the guards gathered up the parchment, holding it across his chest as if it were the Primate's own scepter. The other guard handed over a small box.

Unlike the iron cask that held the tithing coins, this container was made of fine-grained oak, polished to the highest sheen. The titheman removed the lid with a casual gesture, utterly bored by his mundane task.

To a village girl from Silver Hollow, though, the contents of that box were anything but boring. The titheman lifted out a crystal vial, carefully carved to split sunlight into a hundred different prisms. Immediately I thought of the Travelers' piece from the night before.

The crystal vial was filled with a bright purple liquid, as if fresh-pressed wine had been blended with the blue of the noontime sky. The tithing dye was made from the bellies of snails that grew only in the ponds of the Primate's gardens. Rumor said it took a thousand snails to make a thimbleful of dye. The vial held enough to mark the wrists of every person in Silver Hollow three times over.

The titheman produced a stone-handled brush from his oaken treasure box. I knew that the bristles had been fashioned from a yearling colt's snow-white mane, cut and carded and combed by a dozen different workers, so that each individual hair lay in perfect alignment.

"Come then, Keara of Silver . . . Hollow." The titheman's hesitation was obvious, but he ultimately said the correct word. "Offer up your right hand, in service to the Primate."

I braced my fingers against the table. Some tithemen made a mess of tattoos—their hands shook, or they were poor artists. One year my sister Robina's forearm had looked bruised, the ink was so sloppy. I had teased her for days, until Mother made me take my cruelty to Caw.

This titheman was good. His strokes were careful. His design looked braided, as it was supposed to do. I could make out each separate strand in the knot that he painted against the pulse point in my wrist. The dye dried upon contact with my skin, soaking deep immediately.

I didn't realize I was holding my breath until the titheman completed the final line of his design. As always, the stone-handled brush was miraculously clean when he was done. I did not know if the dye had some special property, or if the tithemen were merely well trained not to waste any of the precious stuff.

"Go forth, Keara of . . ." He hesitated before bulling ahead with his final blessing. "Go forth, Keara, and give pride to your Primate, your village, and your family."

"Thank you, lord," I said, barely resisting the urge to poke at my new tattoo.

By then others had gathered on the green. Goody Weaver was tugging her seven sons up to the table, whispering sharp reminders, telling them to stand straight, to look the titheman in the eye. Other villagers drew near.

It seemed, though, that Mother stood apart from everyone. Tears melted in the corners of her eyes, and she swallowed hard when I smiled at her. My voice trembled as I said, "Thank you, Mother."

I wasn't thanking her just for the tithing. I meant everything else—for feeding me and teaching me how to spin, for making sure that I knew the uses of her herbs, for protecting Caw and me beneath her roof. Caw had said she was afraid of losing me, and for the first time ever I felt a hint of that fear myself.

She reached out and tucked a wayward strand of hair behind my ear. "You're welcome, Keara-ti."

And then, because I was still a child for a few days more, because I hadn't yet been presented at Bestius's godhouse, because

Caw was still alive, I threw myself into Mother's arms. She pulled me close, and she rocked me from side to side, as if I were a little girl. I heard her whisper my name over and over again, as if she were praying to the gods, and I was filled with overwhelming sorrow that I would soon be moving away to the Women's Hall.

# Chapter Three

Mother held true to her promise: She made me seedcake when we returned from the green. The rich smell filled our cottage as it cooked on the hearthstone. My sisters drifted over the doorstep at noon, as if they had somehow known Mother was baking. For a while we were a family again, Mother and Robina and Morva and me. We spread thick butter over our cake, laughing and talking as if we were only waiting for Father to return from the vineyards.

But Father was never coming back from the vineyards again.

Mother set out a bowl of sweet redfruit when we had finished our cake. She must have found a vine the day before, when she was wandering the plains in search of her rarest herbs. I consciously told myself not to be greedy with the luscious treat. I remembered to start with one, to eat it all the way down to the pit, with the juice running down my hands, streaking past my new tattoo.

Robina passed her own redfruit from palm to palm, smelling it, but not taking a bite. She was probably saving it for her husband, for Lastor. She did things like that, because she loved him. I wasn't certain that I could ever love a man that much. At least not if I was hungry.

But Robina finally set the redfruit on the table, taking care that it didn't roll onto the floor. When she looked up at us, her eyes were sparkling. "Lastor and I have a secret," she said.

Mother caught her breath, and Morva bit off a little shriek of excitement. I was annoyed that they knew what Robina was going to say, that they understood when I was still ignorant. My oldest sister glanced down at her lap, turning her head to a becoming angle. She looked shy, demure, like the carved wooden statue that sat inside the doorway of Madrina's godhouse. "We're going to have a baby," Robina said. "By the Snow Moon."

The announcement sent Mother barreling around the table; she folded Robina into her arms as if my oldest sister were a newborn herself. Morva sprang to her feet as well, laughing and embracing Robina. I followed suit, only a half step behind the women in my family.

Robina was going to be a mother. I was going to be an aunt.

I was going to hold a little baby, a boy or a girl, an infant who would grow to love me. I would be one of the women who would guide it through the Family Rule, through all the intricacies of village life.

As I added my arms to the pile, I looked at Caw, wondering what he made of the commotion. He thought loudly, *"It's a good thing you're all shrieking now. That will get you accustomed to the noise after the baby is born."*

I started to scowl at him, to tell him he should be more positive. But then I realized there was a sadness beneath his words, a tone I rarely heard from him. Of course. He would never see Robina's child. He would be long gone by the Snow Moon.

I tried not to let that thought ruin our celebration. We all laughed as Mother bustled to the chest in the corner of our cottage. She dug out the nameday dress Robina had first worn, then Morva, then me. The stitches on the garment were impossibly small; flowers tumbled across the precious linen with incredible precision, each one immediately identifiable as a real, specific herb.

Morva insisted she would weave a blanket for the new baby. Not to be outdone, I promised to knit a cap, and soft leggings, too. A Snow Moon baby would need to be protected against the cold. By the time my sisters left our cottage, I was already imagining the oak leaf pattern I would work into the edge of the cap.

The afternoon flew by with a variety of chores. Under

Mother's hawkish eye I scrubbed down our oaken table, using first the harsh brown sand, then the fine white. After that I swept the cottage, working the corners three times to make sure I collected all the grit. I paid special attention to the hearth, digging out the dead ashes and carrying them to the communal pit where others could collect them for soap. Every task left me hotter and sweatier, wishing more heartily for a quick dip in the rushing Silver River.

As I worked, Mother extracted seeds from her dried pods of dead man's hand. Each pod looked like a shriveled finger. As Mother worked, the air filled with the stench of rotting flesh. I knew that the roasted and ground seeds were the strongest defense we had against fever, but I hated when Mother made this harvest.

Caw protested too, flapping his wings inside his cage. *"She should take that mess outside. The stink is enough to make me never want to eat again."*

It wasn't my imagination, then. The stench must be truly terrible if it could drive Caw from food. Nevertheless, I took care to think my reply, knowing that we'd both suffer if I said the words aloud. *"She does what she wants, Caw. If only I could order her to take that to her darkbeast."*

Caw croaked his throaty laugh, and Mother looked up from her work. After a long minute of glaring at both of us, she went back to sorting the smelly seeds.

Finally she left the cottage to wash her hands in our neighbors' trough. The stink would be diluted by all that water. It would have lingered if she had used our own much smaller buckets, but the neighbors' cows would never know the difference.

When Mother returned, she laid out cold seedcake for our supper. I set aside a healthy chunk for Caw. Before I was finished eating, Mother settled her visiting cloak over her shoulders. Bright embroidery danced along the garment's hem. "You'll stay here, Keara? I want to visit with our neighbors. I want to share Robina's wonderful news."

"I'll stay here." I didn't meet her eyes. Instead I scrutinized the tattoo around my wrist, as if I found the painted knot work fascinating.

"I don't want you wandering on the green," she warned.

I shook my head.

"Say it," Mother ordered.

I glanced at Caw's cage. He had taken my lying years before. "I won't go wandering on the green."

Mother's eyes narrowed, but she accepted my words. The sky was already growing dark when she slipped out the cottage door.

I meant to follow the rules. Really, I did. I was grateful to Mother—for paying my head tax, for making me seedcake, for sharing the redfruit. I knew that I needed to be a good girl now, a good *woman* in just a handful of days. Robina's baby was going to look up to me, admire me as an aunt who was kind and wise and who did what she was told by her elders. There was no reason to delay crafting that image for myself.

I might have succeeded in being good if I hadn't heard the Traveler's voice. It was the old man again, the one who had introduced the play about Patrius and the First Primate. His words were loud enough that they penetrated the cottage walls, sharp as arrows. "Our humble Travelers will perform the tale of *Pondera and the Broken Scales*."

Pondera. The goddess of balance. The keeper of harmony. A goddess that I should know much more about, given how often I upset the balance and harmony in Mother's life.

As my hand settled on the door latch, Caw said, *"You told your mother you would not go."*

"I said I wouldn't wander on the green. I won't. I know exactly where I'm going to walk. I won't be wandering at all."

*"I doubt your mother will see things that way."*

I didn't answer. My only other argument was that I had made a *statement*; I hadn't spoken an actual promise. But that was mincing words, whittling them as fine as a baby's eyelash. Caw would never accept such an excuse. And he was the only one listening to me. I closed the door on my darkbeast and slipped into the hot summer twilight.

The Travelers were even more magnificent than they'd been

the night before. Their voices were louder, more sure. Their costumes were brighter. Their story was even more compelling.

The goddess Pondera was visiting a market town, watching over all the goods in the marketplace. A merchant cheated every one of his customers, placing false weights on his scales. He wasn't evil, though. He cheated because he needed coins to clothe his family, to buy new shoes for his youngest daughter, whose feet were chapped and bleeding in the winter cold.

The merchant's crime was discovered by a boy. The boy wore a costume, like all of the Travelers, but he did not wear a mask. Instead his face was bare to the world, his dark eyes huge in his pale face. Even though this was only the second time I'd seen the Travelers, I understood that the boy looked that way so we all would trust him, we all would understand the struggle he undertook.

As I watched, the boy completely ceased to be a Traveler. He became just an ordinary child, someone I would know well if he lived in my village. We would play by the river, squeezing mud between our toes. We would frighten each other on the Night of the Dead, marking grim Mortana's gloryday. We would poke at each other's darkbeasts, hearing the very worst there was to hear about each other.

But this boy was also a stranger, caught up in his tale of gods and of betrayal. He guided the cheating merchant to a home in the town, to a family where two children lay ill. There, a weeping widow counted out her last coppers in hopes of buying herbs to cure her babes. The merchant recognized that some people needed even more than he, and he reformed his practice. He stopped weighting his scales. Pondera watched over all, shedding rain like tears of joy. For raindrops fall on all men alike, on good and evil without discrimination. Thus perfect balance is maintained.

The audience cheered when the play ended, clapping their hands and stomping their feet. I wanted to join in, wanted to share my joy, my excitement. But I knew I needed to get home. I needed to sneak back into our cottage before Mother discovered my disobedience.

I wasn't fast enough. Mother waited for me on our stone threshold.

"I didn't—," I started to say.

She didn't let me get out the rest of the words. Instead she grabbed my wrist and dragged me over to Caw's cage. She looped the old cloth leash over my fresh tattoo, tugging it tight. "Take it to your darkbeast," she spit. She slammed the door as she left the cottage—for the Women's Hall and Morva, or for Robina and Lastor, I didn't know. It didn't matter.

*"It looks as if your mother disagreed with your interpretation of the rules,"* Caw said mildly.

I rubbed at my wrist. The purple dye had begun to itch,

the way it did every year. It would be irritated for a fortnight. Annoyed, I scratched at the painted knot, even though I knew my nails would only make things worse. "She just doesn't want me to have any fun."

*"And that is why she baked you a seedcake?"*

He eyed the table suggestively. We both knew there was one slice left. One slice that Mother had probably meant to be mine, before I disobeyed her. I wasn't about to take it now, though. Not without permission. Not even if Caw begged me for the sweet. I sighed and collected a handful of ripe silberries from the mantel. I passed the treats through the bars of Caw's cage one by one. They were the last of the glistening fruits for the year; I had picked the bushes clean four days before.

*"She wants to keep you close, Keara-ti,"* Caw said after he had swallowed the sweet berries.

"But shouldn't I be learning about the gods? Isn't that what a responsible adult would do?"

*"You aren't an adult yet. Perhaps your mother wants you to focus on lessons closer to home."*

"What can I learn here? Better ways to sweep the floor? To carry ashes? I know how to do everything here."

*"Everything?"*

Of course there were things I did not know how to do. I could never bake a cloud cake as light and fluffy as Mother's. I didn't know how to set prices for goods in the Rivermeet market. I didn't know the precise dosage of every last medicine, the measurements that could mean the difference between healing and death.

I sighed, understanding the criticism inherent in Caw's question. "I have things left to learn. I should have listened better to Mother. I should not have gone to see the Travelers."

*"I take your rebellion,"* Caw said approvingly. *"Forget it. It is mine."*

But Caw was wrong.

For another four nights the Travelers performed on our village green. Each night Mother forbade me to leave the cottage. Each night I crept out anyway. Each night she leashed me to Caw's cage, muttering about how my darkbeast had grown weak, how its time was almost come. Each night I shivered through the darkbeast sensation, the tingling, soaring swoop of a fault taken away forever.

But Caw's magic did not work. My darkbeast did not take my rebellion.

Mother could have wrapped me in a chain from the blacksmith's shed. She could have hobbled my ankles with a length of cloth. She was clearly testing me.

And every night I thought that I was strong enough to complete the test. After all, I loved Mother. I honored her. I respected her.

But I could not skip seeing the Travelers. They called to me like water to a feverish child, like food to an empty belly. I needed them, and I could not keep from breaking Mother's rule.

After the Travelers' sixth night in Silver Hollow, they packed up their wagons. They loaded all of their costumes into great chests. The next day the youngest village children ran after them as they lurched down the road; everyone waved and called farewell until the brightly painted caravan disappeared around a bend in the road. Mother sang a happy tune all morning long.

I was sorry to see the Travelers leave, but I also felt relieved. It seemed as if I was awakening after a long fever, after days and days of poultices and bitter teas and wild, storm-tossed dreams. I never should have let the Travelers consume so many of my waking thoughts. I should have worried about other things. I should have thought about Caw.

After all, the next day was my nameday. The next day I needed to kill my darkbeast.

# Chapter Four

I woke before sunrise. Mother had left the cottage; I was alone on our mattress of lavender and grass. Automatically I looked at Caw's cage, but it was empty, as I had known it would be.

I lay in bed and tried to imagine what life would be like without Caw. I could not remember a time when he was not my closest friend, when he did not know what I was thinking and feeling. He often understood my hopes and dreams and fears before I did. He comforted me when I was frightened or sad, cajoled me when I was cranky or tired.

Certainly, we had spent some time apart. Occasionally I left him in the cottage while I searched for rare herbs in the hills. I often crossed the village green without him, completing urgent errands for Mother without bothering to fiddle with the door to his cage.

We could speak to each other's minds only across a limited distance—about as far as I could see him. Beyond that, I could not hear his wry observations. He could not see what I saw. We could not share our thoughts about the world around us.

But every night of my life, except for those first twelve nights, Caw had watched over me as I slept. Every morning after those first dozen dawns he had been waiting for me to open my eyes. He was as much a part of me as my own eyes, my ears, my nose, and my tongue.

But not now. Not this morning. Not ever again.

As the songbirds started their dawn chorus, I began to hear other noises outside—a whisper here, a giggle there. There was a lot of shuffling, and more than once someone started to ask a question, only to be silenced by others.

Just as I was considering throwing off my quilt and giving up the game, the cottage door burst open. Mother led the group that swept into the room—all of my aunts, my older girl cousins, Robina and Morva, even my ancient grandmother. They sang the Morning Song in laughing voices, not caring about perfect pitch or tone.

Mother filled our painted wooden tub with steaming water. My grandmother should have been the one to draw the bath for me.

That was her honor as the oldest woman in our family, but she was too old to lift the buckets. Last summer she'd had a fit while she was churning butter. Now she was unable to move the muscles on the left side of her body, and she constantly looked like she was frowning. She lived in the Women's Hall, where there was always someone to help her, to tend to her needs.

Nevertheless, Grandmother's moss green eyes—the ones that matched my own—were bright as I knelt in the wooden tub. I let the women sluice water down my back. They wet my hair as well, and they washed it with soap made from rosemary and tallow and ash. They scrubbed my hands and my feet, peeling away the dirt of child's play. My tax tattoo itched fiercely, but I tried not to scratch.

After I was bathed, my sisters presented me with a new gown. The cloth was blue, which was Robina's favorite color. The stitches had been done in green and white, Morva's choice. I would have preferred red, but no one had asked my opinion. I knew better than to complain when they had spent so much time and effort on me.

They wrapped me in an underdress of clean linen, and then they settled the fine gown over my head. My mother made me kneel at her feet, and she combed out my hair, working the snarls from my red-brown curls. One by one my cousins knelt beside us. Each one whispered a nameday greeting and offered up a fresh flower from the fields. I thanked each of them with the proper verse of the Family Rule. My mother smiled as she wove the blossoms into my hair.

When my body and my hair were dressed, I was presented to my aunts. One shaded my cheeks with red. Another outlined my eyes with black. Yet another dotted precious blue—the most costly of all the colors—on my eyelids. The last, the youngest, spread crimson on my lips. I thanked each of them with the Family Rule again, fighting against the nerves that clenched my belly.

Mother squinted as she reviewed me, and I remembered to stand very tall. I looked down at her feet, blinking my painted eyelids like a demure young woman. I turned about when she commanded, stopping after one full revolution.

"Keara-ti," she said at last. That was the last time I would ever hear the endearment on her lips. She would never again call me by the beloved-child version of my name. "You make me proud." I had never heard such words from her. She even sounded loving when she said, "Now it is time to kill your darkbeast."

Every girl did it. Every girl was dressed and pampered on her twelfth nameday. Every girl was taken to Bestius's godhouse, to the small square building in the center of our village.

But I was strange. I was different. I *loved* my darkbeast, loved Caw as if he were the brother I'd never had.

Knowing I could not protest, I gathered up my nameday gift for Bestius. Then I let my family parade me through the village.

Our neighbors stood on their doorsteps, laughing and calling out nameday wishes. I saw Cadi and Finna, who had turned before me. They smiled with honest welcome, anticipating my joining them in the Women's Hall. I had missed them these past several months, missed the easy games we used to play when we were through with all our chores. I would be free to join them soon.

After I killed Caw. That was the only thing I had to do. Kill Caw.

Bestius's godhouse was located in the very center of our village. It was a low, square building, fashioned out of black-stained wooden planks. They mimicked the great slabs of onyx that a richer village would provide to honor the god. A bulging-eyed fly was carved over the doorway, Bestius's sigil. It reminded all visitors that the god embraced darkbeasts of every shape and size.

A village as small as Silver Hollow didn't have its own priest, of course. But for the occasion of my nameday one had come all the way from Rivermeet. He greeted me on the doorstep of the godhouse, standing straight and commanding in his imposing black robes. He must have been hot on that summer day, but I couldn't tell by looking at his face. Instead I saw only a somber old man with wrinkles as deep as the trenches my fingernails were digging in my palms.

Feeling shy, I bowed to the priest, offering up my nameday gift to the god. I had woven the blanket during the winter, using

Mother's backstrap loom and wool dyed black with mardock root. It had taken me three tries before Mother approved my work; I had grown tired of unraveling my mistakes. The gift seemed inappropriate for this summer day, as if I had forgotten my nameday coincided with the Thunder Moon.

Nevertheless, the priest accepted my present with the expected words, smiling and welcoming me into his refuge. I paused on the threshold, looking back at Mother. Expectation shone in her eyes.

She hoped that I would become the daughter she had always dreamed of. She hoped that I would stop being Keara the disobedient, Keara the tardy, Keara the sarcastic. She wanted me to be Keara the meek, Keara the humble, Keara the good daughter. She wanted me to be a woman.

As Bestius's priest led me inside the godhouse, I heard all the village children pressing close to the black walls. They chanted in unison: "Kill the darkbeast! Kill the darkbeast! Kill the darkbeast!"

I had been one of those children dozens of times in the past. I had encouraged others to destroy their pasts, to turn toward their futures. Because I had been one of them, I understood that the children did not chant out of malice. Rather, they merely stated what everyone knew: Darkbeasts served a purpose, and then they died.

"In the name of Bestius," the priest said, "be welcome." He stood between two beeswax candles. Those expensive tapers must have cost Mother a quarter of her earnings from last spring's Rivermeet market. "Your darkbeast awaits you in the inner chamber. Slay your past and look to your future and your life as a woman in Silver Hollow."

At least he knew my village's proper name. He was better than the titheman.

As if in response to that thought, the priest cast his deep-set eyes toward my wrist. He took a silent measurement of my tattoo, noting the brightness of the purple dye. I was safe. I was a good girl. My head tax had been paid.

"Come, Keara. Complete your task, and emerge from the darkness as a woman."

I knew there was some proper response I was supposed to make, something that Mother had taught me to say. But I could not remember it now. I bowed my head instead, whispering thanks with ordinary words. If the priest was offended, he gave no sign. Instead he opened the door to the godhouse's inner sanctuary. He stepped back so that I could pass, and he said, "Be brave." The door latched closed, and I heard the iron lock turn.

The inner room was dark, lit only by a brazier in the center of the floor. Plumes of incense curled into the air, and I sneezed twice. I wiped my nose on the back of my hand, only just remembering not to rub at my painted face.

*"Aye."* Caw laughed. *"That would leave you quite the sight."*

"Caw!" I blinked in the dim light, and I finally made out the glint of his eyes in the darkness. He was trapped in a cage, suspended from the chamber's flat ceiling.

*"Were you expecting someone else?"*

"Of course not."

*"Then don't waste my time with foolish words."*

I shouldn't waste anyone's time with words at all. I should complete my mission. I should take Caw from his cage, close my fingers around his neck, and twist. Instead I said, "It's too dark in here."

*"It's as dark as it is,"* he said, using the practical tone that always drove me mad. *"Did you bring me anything to eat? I've been here for hours."*

"I'm sorry! I didn't think!"

*"You never do,"* Caw said, but he didn't seem too concerned.

All the same, I felt accused of being a glutton, as if I had consumed all of my breakfast, and his, and my family's as well. I said, "I didn't get breakfast either. Stupid rules."

*"The world's an unfair place,"* Caw said. *"You'd appreciate that more if you watched from behind the bars of a cage."*

He made a noise that was the avian equivalent of clearing his throat. It was an expectant noise, a prompt. I understood that he was telling me what to do, reminding me of my obligations in this dimly lit godhouse. "I'm not ready to let you out," I said. "Not yet. You know what will come next."

*"And you're afraid."*

"I am not!"

He hopped down to the floor of his cage, spreading his wings wide. Then he turned to look at me with one shiny eye. *"You look afraid to me. Your cheeks are pale beneath those ridiculous paints."*

"I just wish everything could be different." I wondered how much time had passed. I wasn't sure how long Bestius's priest would wait before he opened the door. I only knew that he expected me to present him with proof I had killed my darkbeast. Then I would fashion Caw's remains into a totem for the house I would eventually share with my husband. The very thought turned my empty stomach. "I can't do it," I said. "I can't kill you."

*"You must."*

"I never asked for this. I never asked for you to take my failings from me."

*"Bestius sent me, though. I came to you, whether you wanted me or not."*

"I was only a baby. You couldn't have known what you were taking on, how difficult I would be. You couldn't have known how many faults I would have."

*"Oh, I knew."* He tilted his head as if he were studying the onyx slab of the altar. As if he were studying our past. *"Is that pride that I hear in your voice?"*

"No." And despite my nerves, I smiled. "You took that one, well enough. What you hear is rebellion."

*"Ah,"* my wise darkbeast said. *"We didn't quite master that, did we?"*

I thought of the Travelers, of their six nights of miraculous shows. "No," I said. "We did not master rebellion."

*"So I failed as a darkbeast after all."*

"No!" My insistence was so sharp it burned my lungs. "You have not failed at anything!"

Caw merely shifted in his cage, fluttering his wings until they kindled like a dark rainbow. *"It is time, Keara-ti. The priest will return soon."*

"I will refuse."

*"You must show him my death."*

"I can't!" How did other children manage? How did they murder their rats and snakes, their toads and tortoises? How did they kill their teachers and their allies, their closest friends in all the world?

*"If you do not kill me, there will be consequences."*

Consequences. I had no idea what Mother would do if I did not kill my darkbeast. Bestius's priest, either. Certainly, no child in Silver Hollow had ever refused—all the adults I knew had been grateful to be rid of their hated companions.

But killing Caw would be like killing a part of myself. I could no more execute my darkbeast than I could cut off my own arm, than I could sever my foot.

Before I could doubt myself, I opened the door to Caw's cage. "Be free," I said.

He looked at me, first with one eye, then the other.

I repeated myself, my whisper harsh. I heard Bestius's priest outside the door. "Be free!"

Caw flew out of the cage as the priest's key turned in the lock. Light flooded through the doorway; the priest was prepared to lead me back into the world, to guide me into my role as a woman among my people.

For just a moment I thought my darkbeast would depart without a whisper of farewell. But then I heard him say, *"I take my freedom. Forget it. It is mine."*

And then he flew through Bestius's godhouse, bursting out the open door and flapping his strong wings to soar high in the sky.

# Chapter Five

Caw's wings caught the priest's head as he flew past, and the man bellowed in surprise. The priest staggered back a step or two, grabbing at the rope belt that cinched his robes into place. Even as he regained his footing, he thundered, "What have you done?"

He grabbed at my wrist with brutal hands, tugging me forward. His fingers closed around my tax tattoo, tightening with fierce rage. The itch of the purple dye flared into a steady burn, but I knew better than to try to pull my arm free. The priest swore by all the gods as he chivied me out the godhouse door.

"Take her," he commanded to Mother. "She is yours."

I wondered if the priest realized he was twisting Caw's customary words. I didn't have time to ask, though. The man glared at me as if I were something vile on the sole of his rope sandal. Then he shoved me out of the godhouse.

He pushed with enough force that I fell to the ground. I scraped my hands and knees and ripped my new blue dress. The gown my sisters had made for me was the most beautiful garment I had ever owned, and now I had ruined it.

Ruined it. Like I'd ruined everything else.

"I'm sorry," I said to Mother, but she only shook her head, glaring at my skinned palms, my ragged knees, my torn garment. My sisters' eyes filled with tears, and my aunts began to whisper among themselves. My cousins stepped back, awe filling their faces. Whispers started at the back of the crowd and rolled to the front, like a summer storm descending from the hills. No one had ever heard of a girl who failed to kill her darkbeast.

"Mother," I said, stepping toward her. She turned her back on me, taking refuge in the gathering of women.

I didn't know what to do.

And so I turned away and walked home, all alone. When I got to our cottage, I removed my torn dress and stripped off my linen shift, replacing both with my customary clothes. I combed the flowers from my hair. I washed the paints from my face. I lay down on the bed, even though the sun was still high in the sky. I turned my face to the wall.

Morva came first. She was closer to my age than any of my other female relatives, closer to the day when she had wrung the neck of her own darkbeast, a nasty, sharp-toothed bat. She crept into the cottage, as timid as a mouse. I barely felt her settle on the edge of the mattress.

"Keara?" she asked. I kept my eyes closed, hoping she would think I was asleep. "Keara-ti? Let us help you make this right." There was a long pause, and then Morva left, quiet and sweet and meek as she always had been. Her darkbeast had had an easy job, taking her failings.

Robina was not as understanding. When she arrived, she strode across the floor, each footstep pounding into the earth like a soldier's boots on the Great Road. She did not sit beside me; instead she positioned herself at the foot of the bed. From her tone I knew that she had set her hands on her hips, that she was squinting, with her chin jutting forward. "Get up, Keara. You must make this right. You must track down your darkbeast and kill him now, before the sun sets."

I didn't answer. I couldn't find Caw even if I wanted to. If he had any sense—and I knew he did—he would be halfway to Rivermeet by now.

Robina sighed in exasperation and grabbed my arm. She hauled me up to a sitting position, as if I were nothing more than a rag doll. "Come, Keara. You don't have a lot of time."

I stared at a spot on the floor, a place where the packed earth was starting to crack. I wasn't trying to be difficult. I just didn't know what to say. I didn't know how I could explain what I had done, why I had done it. Why I wasn't sorry that Caw was flying free, somewhere far from Silver Hollow.

Robina slapped me. My cheek stung, the way it had when we both were children, when Robina would play the mother and strike me if I did not follow her orders. I didn't like obeying her commands then, and I wasn't about to do it now. I wondered how her darkbeast had failed to take her anger, had failed to tame her rage.

"Keara!" she said. "You have to do this. You have to make this right! Find your darkbeast *now* and finish what you started in the godhouse."

I continued to stare at the floor. Eventually, Robina got tired or angry—*more* angry—or bored, and she left.

I sat on the edge of the bed. I knew I was supposed to feel something. Shame, maybe. Or regret. I didn't feel anything, though. Inside, I was a huge cavern of darkness, of nothingness.

Mother was the next person to enter the cottage. She opened the door the way she always did, as if she had every right to cross the threshold. Which, of course, she did. She looked around the room. Fresh loaves of bread were stacked on the table. We were supposed to share them with the village that night, to celebrate my killing my darkbeast. A deep bowl was filled with redfruit, and another overflowed with blackberries, fresh from the summer brambles. There were pitchers of fresh milk, the cream set on top.

Mother selected a smooth round of chestnut bread. She broke it in two, and then she sat beside me. She offered me half, and I took it automatically. Mother nodded and bit into her own piece. As she chewed, I stared at mine. I wasn't hungry. I couldn't imagine ever being hungry again.

Mother didn't force me to eat. Instead she sighed and leaned close. "Keara-ti. You know that Bestius's priest won't let this go." I didn't say anything. I had no idea what the priest would do. "He'll send a messenger bird to Rivermeet. There's an Inquisitor there, one who will come to investigate."

*Inquisitor.* I had seen an Inquisitor ride through Silver Hollow last year, or was it the year before? He'd been a tall man, dressed all in white, shrouded in a cape that swept to his ankles and a hood that peaked high over his head. He had stopped on the village green, asking Goody Weaver if there was an inn where he could spend the night. We were too small a village to have an inn, of course, so he had stayed in Pondera's godhouse. Everyone had brought food and wine, but that supper had been eaten in near silence.

Everyone knew that Inquisitors rode in search of the Lost. Everyone knew that Inquisitors were charged with bringing wandering sheep back to the fold, back to the gods who loved them.

Everyone knew that Inquisitors traveled with the tools of their trade—knives and whips and other holy instruments designed to guide the Lost, to help them find the path to righteousness.

First Primate Kerwen had appointed the first Inquisitors, ordering them to ride through all Duodecia, to bind all people in service to the Twelve. As the Primate's power had grown through the ages, so had the Inquisitors'. There were hundreds of them now, each dedicated to one of the Twelve. The Primate himself watched over the swearing in of Inquisitors, adding royal approval to that of the gods. An Inquisitor was more powerful than a dozen tithemen. A hundred, even.

I could not imagine what I would say to an Inquisitor. I could not imagine how I would explain that I loved Caw, that I could not kill my darkbeast.

Now Mother said, "This isn't just about Caw, Keara-ti. You insulted Bestius himself when you refused to make your offering. You have angered a god."

Certainly, I'd angered a *priest*. I wasn't at all sure that Bestius had any idea what I had done. Didn't a god have better things to do than worry about whether one twelve-year-old girl was killing her darkbeast in some out-of-the-way village in the middle of Duodecia? Couldn't the Inquisitors be put to some better use?

Mother gestured to the bread in my hand. "Come now, Keara-ti. Eat up. And then we'll find your darkbeast. There's been a bond between you for twelve years. We can draw on that. You can make things right."

I couldn't force myself to take a bite.

Mother sighed in exasperation and said, "This is not one of your games, Keara. This isn't just a matter of your breaking *my* rules. It's not that you've embarrassed me in front of the village. It's not that I paid your head tax, only to be rewarded by your stubborn insistence that you know what is best. Listen to me, Keara! You do *not* want to get the Inquisitors involved."

I heard what she was saying, and I understood the truth—the idea of an Inquisitor riding for me was terrifying. But Mother wasn't being completely honest. I saw the nervous glance she cast toward our table. She *did* care what the neighbors thought. She *was* upset that I had let her pay for my tax tattoo.

I stared at the floor until she left.

I don't know how long I sat on the edge of the bed. The sun moved across the sky. The village shifted to its afternoon sounds. Children played after their chores were done, women gossiped, and men joked with one another as they returned to their homes from the vineyards, from the plain, from the hills.

The bread in my hand began to dry out. Not enough that it wasn't good to eat—just enough to hint at the stone it would become. I should not waste bread. I should eat it while it was fresh. It was my favorite, after all, chestnut bread.

The more I stared at it, though, the less real it seemed. The bread lost its meaning, like a familiar word whispered over and over until it turned to nonsense. I must find Caw and kill him so that I could be righteous. Righteous. Righteous. Righteous.

I had no idea what "righteous" meant anymore.

The cottage door creaked open again. Grandmother lurched in, tapping her way forward with her solid oaken stick. She stopped halfway across the room and leaned against the table.

This day had done her no favors. She was much more tired than she had been at dawn, when she had joined in the singing of the Morning Song, tuneless but vibrant. She took several deep breaths, rebuilding her strength.

I wondered what she could possibly say to me, what could ever make a difference. I cared enough to look up from my chunk of bread. I met those moss green eyes that everyone said matched mine.

Grandmother's throat worked. Her tongue lapped out over her lips. She bared her teeth, fighting to speak. And then she made a sound, a wordless groan that sounded like Caw, like a raven in the wild.

I stared at her, waiting for her to try again. She seemed pleased with herself, though. A smile spread over her face, pooling like an egg broken into a hot pan. She nodded at me, as if she meant to assure me that she was right. Then she clutched her stick and made her way back to the door, to the village, to the warm air of a summer evening.

I was alone then. The sun set, but Mother did not return. I suspected she was taking refuge in the Women's Hall, surrounded by the adults who would comfort her, who would remind her that I'd always been a willful child. They would tell her she had done no wrong. None of this was her fault. They would be right.

I waited until I heard the village settle down for the night. Hens were locked inside their coops, safe from foxes and other crafty predators. Cows were milked. Children were called home from the green.

I could picture the night sky turning, the constellations arcing across the dome, telling their stories about the gods. When I was certain that Patrius had stridden above the horizon, I finally stood up. I placed my dried-out chestnut bread on the rumpled quilt. I took a fresh, unbroken loaf from the table, and another one of wheat. I gathered up a round of cheese and some redfruit. There was no way to take the berries. They would be crushed to a pulp in no time.

No one was in the streets as I walked through the village. No one saw me leave the only home I had ever known. No one was able to direct me down the road to the next village, or the next.

I knew where I was going, though. I had to find the Travelers. I had to join them, to convince them they should take me in.

I wanted to journey with them, to participate in the beauty and the power and the glory of the tales they had brought to Silver Hollow.

I did not want to leave my village, but I could stay no longer. I was grateful to Mother for paying my head tax. I loved my family. I appreciated everything they had tried to do for me, the way they had tried to bring me back into the fold, like a sheep that had gone astray. I understood that Mother truly did love me—even when she spoke with an exasperated tone, even when she sighed as if I were breaking her soul.

I loved my family, but I was not like them. I was called to the road. Called to the Travelers.

I turned my back on everything that was familiar, and I took a deep breath.

And then a shadow detached itself from the trees. *"I take your village,"* it whispered. *"Forget it. It is mine."*

The lightness and tingle of darkbeast magic rippled down my spine. For a heartbeat I was certain I was flying, soaring as high as Caw himself. My fingers sparked with energy. How could I ever have considered ending this, giving up the power of our connection?

I swallowed hard, and Caw settled on my shoulder. We started down the road toward our future.

PART TWO

# fear

*I was eight years old, and my father had died that morning. He had been harvesting grapes in the vineyard, carrying his big woven basket on his back. My uncle said that my father had his sharp knife in one hand, that he had just cut a huge clump of fruit. He collapsed with a single wordless cry, clutching at his chest. He fell forward, and all the grapes in his basket spilled onto the ground.*

*"They spilled around him," my uncle said over and over again. "All around him, the grapes spilled."*

*Mother wailed her grief. She tore her apron into ragged strips. She snatched at the silver pin that kept her hair piled on top of her head, and she released the heavy braid that was more gray than black. She retreated into our cottage and rummaged among her herbs and paints, coming out only after she had smudged dangerous black* circles around her eyes. That was the sign of mourning throughout all Duodecia.

That night Mother told me to go to the vineyard and collect the grapes my father had spilled.

"I can't!" I wailed, terrified of the strange-eyed woman in front of me. "There are evil spirits out there. There are ghosts!"

"You will get the grapes! We need every bite of fruit we can harvest! Your father is gone, and things are different now!"

"Tell Morva to go! Or Robina! They can gather the grapes. They aren't afraid of the ghosts!"

My mother's fury cut through the horrid paint on her face. She dragged me over to Caw's cage and tightened the rag leash until my fingers turned cold. "Take your fear to your darkbeast!"

I trembled with terror, imagining the creatures that waited for me outside, under the moonlit sky.

Caw stretched his neck, coming slowly awake. He shifted from foot to foot, blinking sleepily at me. "Perhaps we should consult with the priests about the cause of this earth tremor shaking my cage."

I tried to still my shaking hands by taking deep breaths. "I can't go out there, Caw. She wants me to stand where my own father died. She wants me to touch the grapes he touched just before . . . His ghost will catch me, Caw. I know it will."

"If you gather the grapes, you can feed some to me."

*"Caw!" The thought of him consuming my father's harvest was horrifying.*

*Caw made a chittering sound at the back of his throat.* "Come now, Keara-ti. Your mother only wants to know that her husband did not die in vain. She wants to know that she has food to feed you in the difficult days to come."

*My teeth chattered, and my fear made me peevish. "If she wants the grapes so much, then she should go get them."*

"What do you truly fear?"

*"Ghosts." I whispered the word, as if I were afraid of attracting the undead's attention merely by speaking their name.*

"And you believe your father's ghost would be evil? You believe he would attack you, Keara-ti, the last daughter of his heart?"

*Hearing Caw ask the question, I suddenly felt foolish. Still, I persisted. "It's dark out there. There could be other things. Brigands. Wild animals."*

"And there could be grapes, spoiling on the ground."

*"Will you come with me?"*

"Aye. A night journey for a night bird." *He cocked his head at me as I stood straighter, as I brushed hair off my face with my free hand.* "I take your fear," *he said.* "Forget it. It is mine."

*Immediately I felt the release of Caw's acceptance, the soaring, tingling sensation that meant my darkbeast had freed me from yet another fault. My fingers still hummed as I collected my father's grapes from the vineyard.*

# Chapter Six

Hours later I was tired and hungry and more than a little grumpy with Caw. He could take long rests by sitting on my shoulder as I trudged along the Great Road. Once, I caught him falling asleep, hunching his head down and closing his eyes, and I made a point of shrugging dramatically. He squawked as he fluttered to safety, and then he spent a long time flapping from tree to tree above me, darting ahead, then circling back. I should have been pleased that he wasn't stealing a ride from me. But I was only cranky that he could move so easily, so freely, with such speed.

The longer I walked beneath the brilliance of the full Thunder Moon, the more distant Silver Hollow became. I wasn't measuring only in leagues. Everything about my home seemed to belong to a faraway realm. It was a place where everyone thought differently than I did, where they lived their lives in strange ways.

In Silver Hollow people slept at night, tucked soundly beneath their neat-stitched quilts. In Silver Hollow the Primate's order was preserved, with freshly inked tax tattoos that no one dared to scratch. In Silver Hollow children killed their darkbeasts.

I was never going to belong in Silver Hollow again.

I tried to imagine what Mother would do when she came back to our cottage, when she realized that I had taken food and clothing, that I was truly gone. Would she miss me? Would she cry?

Or would she merely feel relieved? Would she be grateful for my absence, finally freed from the constant need to fight with a stubborn, willful daughter?

Mother *had* paid my head tax, though. She had watched proudly as I entered the godhouse to kill Caw. She had added that last syllable to my name—Keara-ti—added the familiar sound that meant she cared for me. I thought she truly did love me. I hoped she did. Caw said she did. I loved her.

I stumbled at the notion, literally tripping over the toes of my shoes. I *did* love Mother. And I missed her.

But I loved Caw, too. And if I went back to Silver Hollow, I would need to kill him. And I could not do that. Ever.

I squinted at the road in front of me, at the ruts etched deep in the stone. For years, countless wagons had passed along the Great

Road, trundling up this very hill, around the bend that hooked off to the left a thousand paces in front of me.

In my exhaustion it took me several heartbeats to register the meaning of the wagon ruts I stared at. They were *visible* in the growing daylight. The night was nearly over.

It was not safe to stay on the road during the day. Mother might send a search party from Silver Hollow. By now Bestius's priest must have sent a bird to Rivermeet, summoning an Inquisitor.

I forced myself to hurry as I climbed the gentle hill. A copse of trees kept guard over the curve in the road, offering some faint hint of shelter.

I was in luck. A giant oak had fallen earlier in the year, and its wood had begun to rot. The trunk provided protection, a shallow cave that was completely hidden from the road. I dug with my hands, pushing deeper, ignoring the furry scent of mildewing leaves, of moist earth. Only when I was certain no one could see me from the road did I rest my head on my pack.

Caw landed on the ground beside me, looking a silent question with his shiny eyes.

"I'm tired," I said. "I need to sleep."

*"This is the most dangerous day,"* he said. *"This is the day they are most likely to find you, to bring you back."*

"If I keep walking, they'll definitely find me. I'll be lying in the middle of the road, snoring."

Caw made a wordless sound at the back of his throat. He didn't argue, though. There was no way for him to take my fatigue, to own that.

"Wake me at sunset," I said. "We'll be safe until then." I was asleep before he could offer any further protest.

I woke well before sunset. In fact, the sun was high in the sky, shrinking shadows to nothing. Insects vibrated in the summer heat, and my body was sticky with sweat. At first I wasn't sure what had jolted me awake. Then I heard the noise, the one that had vibrated through the ground, through the pack I had used as a pillow.

Hoofbeats.

Certainly, there were plenty of people on the Great Road who were wealthy enough to have a horse. But there was something disturbing about this rapid gallop, something about its perfect rhythm that shot fear through my veins. I ducked low against my fallen tree. My hands scraped through brambles as I dragged a sheltering screen across my face, letting me stay hidden but still look out at the road. I glanced around for Caw, but I could not see him.

I didn't have time to call for him. I didn't remember to *think* at him. Instead I caught my breath and watched an Inquisitor ride by.

He was even more terrifying than I had imagined he would

be. His horse was as black as the mardock roots that Mother charred each fall, preparing her remedy for catarrh. All of the beast—hooves, tail, mane, body—was a single, unmarked shadow, in absolute contrast to the Inquisitor himself.

The man wore the traditional snow-white garments of his station. I could not imagine keeping such clothes clean; I would stain them in a few heartbeats, wiping my hands down the front or stepping on my hem. Not the Inquisitor, though. He was wrapped in perfect clouds, as spotless as the first heartsease that blooms on Midsummer Day.

I had no doubt the Inquisitor was racing to question me about my refusal to kill Caw. Mother would be forced to admit that I truly was Lost, that I had fled Silver Hollow. The Inquisitor would circle back on the Great Road, and he would not stop until he found me.

I started to tremble as I thought of what would happen then. Everyone knew Inquisitors trained with Marius's soldiers, learning how to fight. They worked side by side with Nuntia's messengers, mastering the art of communication. They even absorbed Pondera's lesson, the fine art of creating balance and harmony.

A type of balance and harmony, anyway, devoted entirely to the gods. Devoted to restoring the faith of the Lost, of those who had wandered from the true path of the righteous.

I knew the stories by heart—all children did. Inquisitors

began their work with knives and whips, punishing the fools who fled the gods. They ended their labors with words, though. They talked to the ones who had strayed, wore them down with story after story after story, night after night after night. Everyone said the Inquisitors' words were worse than any physical punishment they administered. The things they said burrowed deep inside the minds of the Lost, repeating themselves forever, like a song that eats into dreams.

In the end Inquisitors always succeeded. They always brought the faithful home. Even if they left the Lost on Mortana's high altar, wrapped in grave-clothes, scented with hyssop, ready for the cold, hard ground. Inquisitors never failed.

I did not blink until the man had ridden past my hiding place. I did not breathe until he disappeared around a distant bend in the road. I did not shift my feet until I could no longer hear his fine black horse pounding out its insatiable rhythm.

*"Enough!"* Caw's voice was loud inside my head. *"Let's get moving."*

I whirled around, squinting into the tree branches until I found my darkbeast. He was nestled on a branch, not too far up, no higher than a man's head. His talons had dug into the soft bark closest to the trunk.

"I can't," I whispered. "Not during the day."

Caw made a wordless sound, something that would have been

a tongue click if he were human. *"Fine. At least get more sleep now. You'll be good for nothing all night long if you sit awake all day and fret."*

I knew he was right. He was my darkbeast. He was always right. Besides, he wasn't wasting my time with jokes about being ravenous; he wasn't begging me for food. He must be serious about the need to protect myself, to rest for a long night of walking.

I lay back down, taking care to cover myself with my cloak, even though it was too warm for the dark green garment. I needed to make myself as difficult to see on the ground as Caw was in his tree.

I couldn't sleep, though. Every time I closed my eyes, every time I told myself to take deep breaths, to empty my mind, I thought of the Inquisitor, of the stark white of his robes against the unbroken black of his horse.

"Caw?" I asked at last, barely whispering his name.

*"You're sleeping."*

"You know I'm not."

*"What, then?"* I heard him shifting in the tree above me, obviously dissatisfied that I had not taken his advice.

"Are all of the Inquisitors that frightening? Are they all as large?"

*"How should I know?"*

"You must have seen them before. In Bestius's godhouse? Before you were bonded to me?"

*"I've only seen the same two Inquisitors that you have—today and last year."*

I was astonished by the admission. I'd always assumed Caw had had a grand life before he was condemned to being my darkbeast. He must have traveled with Bestius's priest along the length of the Great Road, from Lutecia in the north to Austeria in the south. He must have frequented amazing godhouses, ones built to serve thousands of dedicated souls, far grander than our sorry excuse in Silver Hollow.

"Where were you, before you were bonded to me?"

*"I don't know."*

That was such a startling admission that I sat up, letting my cloak slip to the ground. "You don't *know*?"

Caw knew everything. He knew my thoughts before I said them. He knew the rules and the requirements of the world around us. He knew what was right and what was wrong, and why I had so much trouble struggling to do the first and not the second. I could not believe Caw did not know his own past.

As I gaped, I caught a glimpse of him, high up in the tree, shifting from foot to foot as if he were embarrassed. *"I don't have any memory of life before Bestius's priest bonded me to you. In that moment I awoke. I could hear you, of course, and all the other living darkbeasts in the village. But I cannot tell you what occurred before your twelfth day. I cannot say if I was an ordinary raven, or something specially bred in Bestius's godhouse."*

I should have been terrified by that admission. Here I was

on the Great Road, without a plan, without any idea of how I was going to save myself, save Caw. And he had just admitted he was no more powerful than I. He had no more memory, no more knowledge of the world around us.

But somehow I found Caw's words comforting. He and I were on this journey together. Like twins, forever joined against the world, we were going to face whatever challenged us. I settled back into the leaf mold beneath the tree, taking care to cover myself completely with my cloak. "Wake me, then, if you see another Inquisitor."

*"You can be sure I'll do that,"* he said. And then I was finally able to fall asleep for what remained of the day, trusting to my companion to keep me safe.

For three nights after that I walked. I left the road often—not only when thoughts of the Inquisitor spooked me, but for other travelers as well. It was easiest to hide from everyone, to treat everyone as the enemy. My fear did not care who roamed the road; anyone could destroy me.

Caw helped protect me, of course. He flew ahead in the darkness, letting me know when I was coming near other people. Everyone else on the Great Road rested at night. They gathered around well-trimmed fires, sharing food, sleeping. I gave them all a wide berth.

Both times that I came to a village, I longed to run through, to pound past the darkened cottages as fast as I could. But I forced myself to slow my pace, to amble as if I didn't have a care in the world. There were plenty of reasons for a girl to be walking in the middle of the night—she could be lost, or on a collecting trip to gather valuable herbs, or traveling to the Rivermeet market for her first time ever, alone.

There was absolutely no good reason for a stranger to run through a village after dark.

On the fourth night I arrived at another hamlet. This one was larger than Silver Hollow, three times its size at least. The sun had set well before I came to their godhouse for Pondera. The familiar circular structure called to me—I knew it would have clean linens and straw mattresses, cool water and fresh food for weary travelers.

Pondera was not my friend, though. Not now. Not when I had ignored her fellow god. Not when I had defied Bestius's edict to kill Caw.

I started to duck into the shadows of a convenient clump of trees so that I could wait for everyone to fall asleep before I continued down the road. But then I heard laughter—children, their excitement floating high on the breeze. Beneath the joyous sound came the skirl of a flute and the steady beat of a sheepskin drum.

I had caught up with the Travelers.

My heart pounded as I crouched beneath an oak tree. I tried to steady my breathing, forcing myself to chew slowly on my last crust of chestnut bread. As I gnawed the hard stuff, I ordered myself to calm down, to stop jumping at every new sound. I no longer had any reason to be afraid. I had reached my destination. I could present myself to the Travelers and ask to accompany them. No Inquisitor would ever think to look for me with the troupe. I would be safe by morning.

When I could breathe without choking, I edged into the village. I darted from shadow to shadow as I made my way toward the green, toward the Travelers' stage. Caw flapped behind me, snagging a perch on the eaves of one cottage, on the chopping block in front of another. I longed to push my way to the front of the crowd, to jostle for the best view. But it would not do to attract attention before I had secured safe passage with the company. I should content myself with listening to the performance instead of watching it.

"Caw," I whispered. "Take a high perch. Tell me if you see anyone paying too much attention to me."

*"You should wait,"* he said. *"Speak to the Travelers outright after their show. No one likes a sneak."*

"I'm not a sneak!"

As if to prove I wasn't lying, I took a few steps closer to the stage, finally huddling in the shadow of a water trough on the edge of the green. I closed my eyes, the better to concentrate on the voices coming from the stage. They had already introduced their tale, one of the oldest: *Nuntia and the Rainbow.* The woman playing Nuntia had a strong, mellow voice. Her words cascaded over the crowd, carrying us along as if she truly were a divine messenger. My heart lifted, and I longed to follow her anywhere, everywhere. I would give all I had to accompany the Travelers down the Great Road.

At the end of the play Nuntia offered the Primate's most loyal general a drink that would seal the message she'd brought to him from all the Twelve. The goddess announced she was brewing heartsease tea, and the general proclaimed the drink sweet, a blessed omen for all the years of his service to the crown.

He was wrong, though.

Certainly, heartsease blossoms *smelled* sweet, but a tisane brewed from the flowers was bitter stuff. I should know—Mother made me drink it when I could not fall asleep. She said it helped, even though it never really made me tired. At least I had learned to pretend to get drowsy so that she would not make me drink more.

Of course, that one misstep in the Travelers' performance did not make me lose respect for them. In fact, I wanted to draw closer, to hear more of Nuntia, more of the general. I wanted to commit every word they said to memory, to master each line so that *I* could be the one on the next stage. Surely there must be a role for me—as a page in the general's army, as an acolyte in one of the godhouses. . . .

The play ended with Nuntia weaving her rainbow across the sky. She promised all mankind to bear their messages to the other gods forever, so long as all men, women, and children held true righteousness inside their hearts. The entire village burst into applause as her silk banners billowed in the flickering torchlight—the red and orange of fire, the yellow and green of grass, the blue of a summer sky, and the violet of sunset. The lengths of silk shimmered across the stage, and then they dissolved into a new shape—a fine-limbed mare, the symbol of Nuntia. The cloth held its shape for a dozen heartbeats before it drifted to the stage.

Slowly, still enchanted by the magic of the play, I backed away from the Travelers and made my way to the far end of the green, where they had made their camp. I should study their wagons, educate myself about their ways. I should learn everything I could so that they would accept me when I asked to join their ranks.

As I ducked into the shadows beneath one of the Travelers' carts, my heart pounded in my ears. I barely heard Caw's wings flap above me. I assumed he was taking up a lookout position. I caught my breath, listening for anyone close by, and then I darted toward the next cart.

There were eight wagons in all, each more brightly painted than the last. They were covered with images of magical beasts and swirling plants, with gold borders that glistened in the moonlight. The largest one was in the center, sheltered by its fellows. Three steps led to its elaborately decorated door.

That was where I could find the information I needed. That was where I could learn about the people I longed to call my own. I caught my breath and counted to ten before I dared to cross the circle. I placed my foot on the first step. The second. I lifted my hand, ready to work the hasp of the door.

And I almost screamed when a hand clamped down on my shoulder. "Where do you think you're going?"

# Chapter Seven

I tumbled from the stairs as I fought to twist free, lashing back and forth like a fresh-caught fish. My struggles were worthless, though. I was shoved to the ground, and a bony knee knifed between my shoulder blades. My captor slipped a rough rope over my hands, cinching the hemp tight around my wrists.

I wanted to scream, but I knew I must remain silent. I dared not bring the villagers running. I dared not call attention to myself, not now, not in the dark of night. Not before I could convince the Travelers to take me with them, to keep me safe from Inquisitors.

Trying to hold fast to my bigger plan, I let my body fall limp. I stopped fighting altogether. I let my captor turn me around, take hold of my chin, tilt my head to a sharper angle in the moonlight and the straggling glow of the torches from far across the green.

And when I saw who had caught me, I almost shouted in astonishment. It was the boy, the one I had seen on the Travelers' stage in Silver Hollow. He had played an innocent there, a child who taught his elders the just ways of Pondera. Now, though, he looked nothing like a child—he was angry and rough, clearly determined to protect his people from an outside threat. From me.

"Let me go!" I whispered. He looked to be my age. He should understand that I didn't mean him any harm, that I would never hurt the Travelers.

"What are you doing here, sneak thief?"

"I'm not a thief!"

He laughed harshly. "Then you admit you're a sneak?"

Even in my mortification I thought of Caw. He had told me not to sneak, but I had ignored him. Once again my darkbeast had been proven right. I hoped I would get a chance to apologize to him.

The boy poked me with his toe. "Go ahead. Say it. Say 'I'm a sneak.'"

I glared at him.

After a long wait he shrugged, and then he used harsh hands to drag me to my feet. "All right, then. Don't say anything to me.

You'll talk to Taggart, though. As soon as the revels are ended, he'll get the truth from you."

Revels. I did not know what he meant by that. And I had no idea who Taggart was. But I was certain to find out. The boy shoved me toward the wagon. When I resisted climbing up the three steps, he planted his hand in the small of my back and pushed.

"So, you were willing to sneak in, but now you won't walk into a Traveler's home, invited?"

Embarrassed, I held my head high and climbed the stairs into the cart. As soon as I saw a victorious smile on the boy's lips, I wished I hadn't. I shouldn't have let him manipulate me so easily.

It was hot inside the wagon. The air smelled of exotic spices, cinnamon and anise and other scents too rare for me to name. An intricately carved iron lantern hung from the center beam, higher than my head. The boy wasted no time reaching for a crooked tool and working open the lamp's door. The orange-gold light of a tallow candle flooded the room.

The far wall, the front of the wagon, was made up as a bed. Bolsters were strewn across a mattress, great blocks of fabric stitched with a frenzy of thread—crimson and sapphire and emerald. To my right a desk folded down from the wall. Even at a glance I could see that it was intricately made, with a dozen locked compartments. Each of them could fold into the side of the wagon, hidden away as soon as the cart started jolting down the road. A massive trunk was lashed to the wall on my left; I could easily have lain flat on the bottom of the container. Other boxes were bound to the walls, hinting at great wealth and even greater secrecy.

In the center of the space four chairs surrounded a painted table. The boy pushed me toward the closest seat, taking a moment to loop the rope that bound my wrists around the back of the chair. I tugged away by reflex, and I discovered that the furniture was bolted to the wagon floor, safe and secure for traveling down the Great Road.

"What's your name?" the boy demanded.

I closed my lips, rebellious as ever.

"You might as well tell me. We'll have Pondera's priestess in here soon enough. She'll pass judgment on you, and you'll have to tell the truth."

Pondera, the goddess who maintained balance. What if the priestess had heard about my rebellion? What if she knew there was a girl from Silver Hollow who had refused to slay her dark-beast? What if she knew about Caw?

Caw. I had ordered him to keep watch as I approached the wagon, but he had given no warning of my captor. Did that mean he was hurt? Frightened? Or merely gloating that he had been right and I had been wrong? I reached out with my thoughts, pushing to find him in the night. *"Caw?"*

Silence.

I could not tell if he was beyond the range of our communication or if he was refusing to answer. It would be like him to teach me a so-called lesson by keeping silent now.

I squared my shoulders and stared straight ahead. If I could only figure out how to plead my case, how to make this boy understand. . . . If I couldn't even speak with someone my own age, how was I ever going to get the older Travelers to accept me?

I had plenty of time to ponder that question while I sat in silence, trying to ignore the ache in my shoulders as my arms protested being bound behind me. I also pretended not to see the boy who sat beside me. He made no secret, though, that he was studying me. He squinted intently, as if he were memorizing the tangle of my hair, the glint of my eyes.

A long time later the wagon door finally opened. The night air was cool against my face, and an unexpected shudder convulsed my spine. I forced myself to sit up straight, to raise my chin in pride. In defiance, I was certain Mother would have said.

I found myself staring at the old man who had announced the Travelers' plays in Silver Hollow. "Well, well, well," he said in a voice that filled the wagon. "What have we here, Goran?"

The boy—Goran—leaped to his feet. "I found her outside your wagon, Taggart, sneaking up the stairs. I think she planned to steal from you, then hide your things in her cottage until we travel down the road."

Taggart nodded slowly, lowering himself into the chair opposite me. I could not keep from staring at his face, at the lines carved deep in his flesh. His beard curled like heavy smoke, twining around the same intricate iron necklace he had worn in Silver Hollow. In the candlelight his eyes looked black; they were sharp and piercing.

"She won't be carrying anything to her cottage," he said, and the words sounded like they'd been dragged over a gravel streambed. "Her home is five days back. This one is from Silver Hollow."

How did Taggart know where I came from?

"What is your name, girl?" he demanded.

"Keara." I had to clear my throat twice before I could get out the two syllables.

"And how old are you, roaming the Great Road alone?"

How old was I? The answer was easy—twelve. But twelve was too young to travel alone. Twelve was barely a woman. If I was twelve, I should be home in Silver Hollow, safe inside the Women's Hall. But how far could I stretch the truth? "Fourteen," I said, hoping I had not hesitated too long.

Taggart merely glared.

"Fourteen!" I insisted, grateful now that Caw had not joined me inside the wagon. If I had been accompanied by my living darkbeast, I could never have lied about my age. "I've always been small for my years." I had to change the subject. I had to lead him away from dangerous speculation about my height, about the plain cut of my clothes, which were obviously meant for a child and not a young woman. I pushed all of my fear into a simple declaration: "I want to come with you. I want to be a Traveler."

"What?" That was Goran, sounding incredulous. Taggart merely lowered his head and stared at me down the long slope of his nose.

"I want to learn your . . . revels," I insisted. The word sounded foreign on my tongue, but Goran had used it, and I would too.

"Our *revels*!" Taggart exclaimed. "And what do you know of those?"

I couldn't answer because I wasn't certain what they were.

Taggart nodded, though, as if I had spoken aloud. "And what do you know of the gods, little one?"

"I know the Twelve, and all that they control. I can name them, and their sigils, and I can recognize their godhouses, even the ones we don't have in Silver Hollow."

"Their sigils," Taggart said solemnly. "Venerius. What is his?"

The god of the hunt. That was easy. "A dog."

"Incorrect." Taggart spoke the word as if he were Pondera herself, passing judgment on me.

"What?" I would have jumped out of my chair if I had not been bound to it. "Of course it is!"

"Nuntia," he demanded, as if I hadn't spoken.

"Her sigil is a horse." I had seen it on the Travelers' stage that very night. Even now I could picture how the silk banners had shaped the animal.

"Incorrect again. Mortana."

"A snow-white she-raven!" I clenched my hands into fists, daring the old man to contradict me. I knew ravens, knew them well enough that anger was washing away all fear of the Traveler before me.

The old man leaned back in his chair. "Goran, fetch Pondera's priestess." His eyes remained fixed on me. "Tell her we have a liar on our hands. A liar who needs an Inquisitor to teach her the way of the gods."

"No!" I shouted before Goran could take a step toward the door. Fear shot through me, acrid as charred bread. I had to avoid the Inquisitor. My escape from Silver Hollow depended on that—my escape, and Caw's life. "If you send me away, I'll never tell you the error in your play!"

Taggart stopped the boy with a curt wave of his hand. "Error?"

"In the story you performed tonight. *Nuntia and the Rainbow.*"

"We have no error." He leaned forward as he said the words. I could smell applemint on his breath; he must have chewed fresh leaves before he moved among the village people. That was one of Mother's tricks when she worked in the marketplace.

"You do," I insisted. "But if you bind me over to Pondera, you'll never know your failing."

Taggart's voice froze. "I know every word of that revel, girl. There is no mistake."

Revel. Of course, that was the Travelers' word for their plays. I had been foolish not to understand that before. I shrugged as best I could with my hands still tied behind my back. "Fine. Make your mistakes. Some other villager may tell you the truth one day. Unless they all just walk away, not trusting any of your revels because they've found the fault in one."

The old man's eyes narrowed, as if he could read the very thoughts inside my skull, hear my inner speech as clearly as Caw. His lips pursed, and his right index finger tapped against the table, steady and patient.

I prayed to all the gods that he could not make out the terrified hammer of my heart. I forced myself to meet his gaze, certain that if I backed down now, I would never have another chance to join the troupe.

"Very well," he said at last. I heard Goran squeak out a wordless protest. "What is the error you think you found?"

"If I tell you, you must let me travel with you."

"You think to bargain like Aurelius himself!"

The god of wealth. His sigil was an ermine. But I had nothing to gain by naming truths about the gods. I had only one thing to trade, one morsel of knowledge. If Taggart chose not to learn, I was doomed.

"All right," he said at last. "You may join us as we journey to our next performance, but no farther."

Something was better than nothing.

"Heartsease tea," I said promptly. "It is not sweet like the scent of the flower. It is bitter as mudroyal. And the taste lasts twice as long."

For a moment I did not think Taggart would believe me. I could see him think through the words of the revel. His lips moved as he got to the line, to the specific rhyming couplet. He repeated it to himself, once, twice, a third time.

"Ha!" he exclaimed at last. "Nesson changed the line. On Midsummer's Eve, it must have been, to mark the blooming of the flower." He laughed, long and hard. "For weeks we've had it wrong. I thank you, little one."

"Then I can join you? On the road?"

"Aye. I stand by my promises. You can go with us to Rivermeet."

It was something. By the time the Travelers were ready to leave Rivermeet, I would find another way to make them need me. For now, though, I remembered my manners enough to say, "Thank you."

I knew I should sit quietly then. I should make it easy for Taggart to keep me by his side. I should disappear into the four walls of the wagon, make myself invisible. But I could not keep from saying, "If you please, sir. The sigils. I was right."

The old man slammed his hand down on the table, making the entire wagon shudder. "Goran?" he asked, as if the boy were still an active part of our conversation.

Goran answered immediately. "Venerius's sigil is a chestnut hound. Nuntia's sigil is a bay mare."

"Details," Taggart said, nodding his approval at Goran's recitation. "Details are important, girl. Details make the story."

He might be right. Nevertheless, I had to protest. "But Mortana? What was wrong with my answer about Mortana? I could not be more specific. Her sigil *is* a snow-white she-raven."

Taggart nodded. "You were right about that one. I just wanted to see what you would do if I threatened you. If I sent Goran for the priestess."

I thought about protesting. I thought about telling him he had broken his own rules. He had lied to me.

But there was nothing to be gained by being difficult. That much I had learned over the years, taking my challenges to my darkbeast. That much Mother—and Caw—had finally succeeded in teaching me.

The old man raised his eyebrows when I stayed silent, but then he waved a hand at Goran. "Go ahead, boy. Untie her. And bring us all a bowl of redfruit. Speaking the revels is hungry work, and I daresay our vagabond here will eat a bite or two."

Unbidden, my stomach growled. Goran actually laughed as

he undid the complicated knot that had kept my hands cinched behind me. I couldn't blame him, really. I almost laughed myself. Taggart said to Goran, "And bring some bread, too. One of those chestnut loaves, along with some cheese."

I actually sighed in hungry anticipation as Goran opened the wagon door. The sound froze in my throat, though, as disaster flew into the wagon.

Disaster, in the form of Caw.

He aimed directly at me. He settled on my left shoulder with a flap of his wings and a twist of his neck. It was obvious to anyone with two working eyes that Caw was my darkbeast.

It was obvious I had lied to Taggart. I could not be fourteen years old. If I were fourteen, I would have killed Caw two full years earlier.

Fear paralyzed me. I had no way to explain Caw. I could not justify the presence of my darkbeast.

# Chapter Eight

In the end, though, Caw was not my undoing.

Taggart merely waved Goran on his way, telling the boy to hurry with our food. Then the old man stared at my dark-beast, seeming to count each of Caw's midnight feathers in the golden light of the tallow candle. It seemed as if Taggart read some secret in my raven's sparkling eyes.

"Fourteen years," he said to me at last, shaking his head. "Do not lie to me again, Keara. If you do, I'll leave you at the nearest godhouse, bound and gagged, and I'll never look back."

I nodded, afraid to trust my voice. Caw chortled gleefully inside my head, *"He takes your lying. Forget it. It is his!"*

I shrugged hard enough that Caw had to ruffle his feathers

for balance, and then I said to Taggart, "I won't lie to you again." I regretted that I could not insist on a similar vow from him.

Goran returned soon enough with food and drink, which all of us enjoyed. I was fighting to swallow my yawns when Goran finally showed me from Taggart's wagon, guiding me by moonlight toward another one of the brightly painted carts.

Fires were lit all around the Travelers' camp, half a dozen carefully tended blazes. Each bright circle was surrounded by a handful of dark shapes. I realized that the Travelers slept under the stars, wrapped in blankets as colorful as the bolsters I had seen inside Taggart's wagon.

The notion made my heart beat faster. The night hid dangers—beasts and strangers, even if there were no true ghosts. As if in response to my panic, Caw chose that moment to take wing. Maybe he was trying to remind me how he had taken my fear years before. Maybe he was just ready to seek out his own bed for the night.

I desperately hoped he was flying only as far as the trees on the edge of the green.

Goran crossed to one of the shadows on the ground and nudged it with his toe. When that action produced no response, he leaned forward and whispered, "Vala!"

I could not make out any words in the sleeper's mumbled response.

"Vala!" Goran said again. He squatted down by the end of the shadow that was closest to the fire. When I blinked hard, I could resolve the shape into a person's head. "Wake up." He shook a blanketed shoulder. Reluctantly the shape shifted, and the shadow rose to a sitting position. Another hard blink, and I could see that Vala was a girl, one who looked to be about my own age.

"Wha?" She glanced around with heavy-lidded eyes.

"Taggart says you're to watch over a new girl. Her name's Keara. She's with us till Rivermeet."

Vala squinched up her face, as if she could not comprehend what Goran was saying. Nevertheless, she shifted beneath her blanket, gesturing to the pack she was using as a pillow. "Mmm," she said in my general direction. She probably thought she was forming words, but she had reclined and was asleep before I could ask her to clarify.

"Go ahead, then." Goran nodded toward the makeshift pallet. "Till the morning."

He darted away in the darkness before I could respond. He was probably just relieved that *he* didn't need to share a blanket with the new girl. At least I had my own pack to cushion my head, and a cloak to gather close.

*"Caw,"* I thought as Vala started snoring softly beside me. I spoke with my mind so that I would not disturb the girl beside me.

*"I am here."*

*"Good. Stay close."*

*"That depends. Do you have treats?"*

I was long out of chunks of dried apple. If I'd been a considerate child, I would have saved Caw a few bites of redfruit from my late-night feast with Goran and Taggart. But that was ridiculous. My free-flying darkbeast could harvest all the redfruit he wanted; it was ripe on the summer vines. *"I'll see what I can find for you tomorrow,"* I promised.

He harrumphed, and I sensed him settling on a branch, ruffling his feathers in displeasure. I didn't have anything else to say to him, though. I had thought his name only to confirm that he was close by. I needed to know my darkbeast had not abandoned me.

Soon enough, I slept.

I woke as the sun crested the horizon, but I forced myself to lie perfectly still until I heard Vala's breathing change, until I was certain she was also awake. Then I muttered to myself, pretending to rise up from my dreams. I stretched as thoroughly as Pondera's cat, taking my time before I sat up beside the cold ashes of the previous night's fire.

Vala was staring at me.

She was as beautiful as some princess out of legend. Her hair hung loose about her oval face—great cascades of night black curls. Her eyes were so dark they seemed to be all pupils. Her skin was bronzed, as if she'd spent long summer days traveling the Great Road.

Which she probably had done.

"Good morning," I said when the silence started to feel uncomfortable. "I'm Keara. Thank you for letting me share your blanket."

Before Vala could answer, I heard the flap of wings, and Caw took his customary place on my shoulder. He cocked his head to one side and studied my companion with all the intensity I longed to employ but could not, for politeness' sake. I waved a hand at him and said, "This is Caw."

Vala nodded, and she finally found her voice. "Good morning." The two words made me think of honey glinting in noontime sunlight. Vala was obviously well trained by the Travelers; she had mastered their incredible vocal control.

Before I could think of something else to say, Vala reached down for a basket nestled in the grass. Her hands seemed accustomed to their task as she pried off the woven lid. Her jaw hardened before she reached inside, and her throat bobbed with barely masked disgust. She flexed her fingers and pulled out a misshapen black lump. "This is Slither. She'll warm up soon."

She shoved her darkbeast toward me.

Slither. A snake. I fought the urge to back away, to dash the creature onto the grass. I had always hated snakes, the way they rippled on their bellies, the way their jaws unhinged so that they could swallow their soft prey whole. I thought a quick prayer of gratitude to Bestius for sending Caw to be my darkbeast, instead of some horrible snake.

But it was rude to ignore Slither. I forced myself to look into the animal's lidless eyes. "Good morning, Slither," I said. I couldn't keep from leaping back, though, when she flicked her tongue in wordless reply.

Vala twined the nasty creature around her wrist. I could tell she didn't like the snake any more than I did. Vala was like most children. She hated her darkbeast. Nevertheless, she explained, "When the mornings are cool, I need to give her some of my warmth. After a while she can hunt for her own food."

I nodded. It wasn't Vala's fault she was bound to such a hideous creature.

As if she could read my mind, Vala said, "My nameday is coming soon. I'll offer Slither to Bestius on the night of the Harvest Moon."

I didn't blame her for sounding eager. I would be eager too if I had spent nearly twelve years bound to a snake.

I managed not to dart a glance toward Caw, not to give any hint about my own nameday. Slither darted out her tongue as if she were testing my silence for truthfulness, and I barely choked back a yelp.

"So," Vala said. "Goran said you travel with us until Rivermeet?"

"Yes. Longer, if I can convince Taggart to keep me." At her curious glance I explained: "I'm from Silver Hollow, but I don't want to go back there. I want to see every corner of Duodecia."

Vala nodded as if my desire made perfect sense. In fact, it probably did to her. She was accustomed to journeying throughout the primacy. She had probably never spent more than a fortnight in any one place. She gestured with the hand that wasn't bound by Slither, taking in the entire circle of Travelers' wagons. "You've chosen a good time to join us. We can use all the able bodies we can find."

"Why?"

Before answering, Vala climbed to her feet and started to fold her blanket. I helped, taking care to keep my fingers away from her fat reptilian bracelet. Vala nodded approvingly and said, "To help with the crying."

"Crying?" I probably looked as confused as I sounded.

Vala nodded. "In the villages along the road. We spread the word about the revels. Tell the people what they'll see if they follow us to a larger town. Announce the revel once we get there."

"Oh," I said. "Crying." I remembered listening to the Travelers the day they arrived in Silver Hollow. I'd heard snippets from their revels, a few of their funniest jokes, hints of the magic in their tales. Now that I thought about it, I realized I had even seen Vala—although her curls had been tamed into a plait then.

Now she raised a single eyebrow, and I immediately promised myself I would learn the trick. "That's the best way to fill our coffers," she said. "Get all the people to attend, night after night. It's especially important to cry the bigger villages, like Rivermeet. We need to gather folks from both sides of the river. Aurelius willing, we'll even get people from Eastmill to cross the Floating Bridge."

"Of course," I said, as if I'd known there was an Eastmill. As if I'd ever heard of a floating bridge.

Vala leaned close to share a conspiratorial smile. "The real fun starts after we leave Rivermeet."

"Why?" I didn't want to think about leaving Rivermeet. I didn't want to imagine being left behind, stranded with Caw and at the mercy of the Inquisitors.

Vala's eyes glinted. "After Rivermeet we'll start to rehearse for the cath."

"What is the cath?"

Vala stared at me as if I were a simpleton, a child so ignorant I had never even heard about the healing strength of bitterroot. "The cath is the Primate's contest!" When I continued to look mystified, she explained. "It opens the Autumn Meet, in Lutecia. Every Traveler troupe competes before the Primate—the Primate, and a group of priests and priestesses, one for each of the gods. They choose the best revel, and the company that wins travels free throughout Duodecia for five full years. No titheman. No paying for tax tattoos."

Five full years. I stared at the violet knot painted on my wrist, trying to envision what five years would mean to Mother. I imagined all those copper coins stacked on our wooden table. On *her* wooden table, I corrected myself sternly. I wasn't going back to Silver Hollow ever again.

I tried to picture the spectacle of the cath. "Does every troupe perform the same revel?"

"Each company plays the revel they do best. Most choose a Holy Play, of course. But nine caths ago our troupe won with a Common Play, with *Ailin and the Spider*."

I heard the boast behind her words, the pride that her Travelers had won, and in such an unconventional fashion. There were dozens of Common Plays, of course, scores of funny stories about ordinary men and women. But I could not imagine any of them being good enough to best a Holy Play. The twelve Holy Plays were ancient, each devoted to a specific god. The Holy Plays, with their constant words, their unchanging lessons, held a special type of magic.

"What revel will you do this year?"

Vala shrugged. "We don't know yet. Taggart will decide. He'll tell us after Rivermeet, and then we'll rehearse for the cath in all the northern villages. We'll be perfect by the time we reach Lutecia."

I was a little cowed by her vehemence. "When is the cath?"

"On Primate Hendor's nameday."

The Hunter's Moon, then. At least I knew that much, ignorant villager that I was. The Travelers would compete for their prize in less than three months. I folded my fingers into fists. I must be with the Travelers when they stood before Primate Hendor.

Obviously unaware of my thoughts, Vala wrinkled her nose and set her palm on the ground. "Ugh," she said as the black snake unwound from her wrist. "She's finally warm enough to feed." I fought down a fresh shiver of fear as the snake disappeared in the grass.

*"Don't be foolish,"* Caw thought as he shifted on my shoulder. *"She's only a darkbeast. Like me."*

*"Not like you,"* I thought back. *"Not at all like you."*

*"Nonsense! That poor snake is exactly like me. She's starving!"* He leaned to one side, flapping his wings feebly, as if he barely had the strength to maintain his post on my shoulder.

Vala looked concerned. "Is your darkbeast all right?"

I gave Caw a sharp glance, wishing I had already mastered Vala's single raised eyebrow. "He's fine. Just hungry. I usually give him a portion of my food."

Vala shook her head slowly. "Bestius save me, I cannot wait for my nameday. I cannot wait to be free."

I struggled for something to say, something that wasn't a lie. I had dreaded my twelfth nameday ever since I first understood what Caw's fate would be.

Vala seemed not to notice my discomfort, though. Instead she loaded her voice with hearty enthusiasm, employing all the skills of a Traveler projecting happiness from the very back of a stage. "Come on, then, both of you! There should be plenty of porridge at the main fire. My father is the camp cook, and he promised to save the last silberries for me, Recolta be blessed. I'll share them with you if you hurry!"

*"Aha!"* Caw said. *"This pious girl is useful already! Porridge. Silberries. What more can a starving darkbeast ask for?"*

*"We don't* use *our friends,"* I thought back sharply, but I almost laughed as well. Caw would break any rule, ruin any lesson, if he thought he might find a choice bit of food. To Vala I said, "Thank you," loading the words with sincerity.

Vala grinned. "My pleasure! And after I teach you how to cry, you must tell me about life in your village!"

I nodded, a little bemused by the notion that there could be anything noteworthy about life in Silver Hollow. But then I remembered the heartsease tea and the correction I had made for Taggart the night before. I *did* know things, things of value to the Travelers. I laughed at the memory of the old man's expression as he recognized the error in the Nuntia revel.

Vala joined her laughter to mine, and I realized I had made my first friend among the Travelers.

# Chapter Nine

I settled into life with the Travelers as if I'd been born to it. Which, in a way, I had been. Life on the Great Road wasn't all that different from life in Silver Hollow. I was expected to gather firewood, to carry water from the local well, to help with cooking, with cleaning, with the thousand little things that made a small community function.

*"Not a lot of darkbeasts,"* Caw complained eight days after we'd joined the Travelers.

"Not a lot of children," I replied.

*"We'd be happier in Austeria. There'd be more people like us."*

There'd be more treats, he meant. More food at the Travelers' home base. Vala had explained that Austeria was where all the Travelers lived when they weren't journeying on the Great Road, when they weren't traveling to the cath. Her description of Duodecia's great southern port city had immediately captured Caw's attention. He pestered me at least three times a day, trying to convince me to turn around and head south. I was pretty sure he just liked the idea of sitting on one of the tall boat masts. Or maybe he wanted to add fish to his diet.

"I'm happy right here," I said. And I was. There were thirty-seven of us on the Great Road. Vala said that twice as many Travelers had stayed behind in Austeria—mostly children, and the oldest Travelers. Except for Taggart, the elderly were content to ease their bones in true buildings instead of wagons, to warm themselves in front of constant hearths instead of flickering campfires. I, on the other hand, was happy to be jolted in a wagon, to have one side of my body scorched by a campfire while the other grew chilled in the night. I loved being on the Great Road.

Caw wasn't willing to give up. *You could learn all the revels if we went to Austeria.* According to Vala, the troupe members who stayed behind performed revels on the glorydays of each of the gods, raising money to support the Travelers on the road.

"I'm learning all the revels here." And I was. At least, I was listening to the Travelers recite their rhymes. And I was becoming intimately familiar with the costumes for each production.

When I had watched the revels in Silver Hollow, I'd been

astonished by the rich robes, the painted masks, the elaborate luxury of every garment. I had never considered how much work each took to maintain.

Every morning there was a knee-deep pile of mending to complete. Hems came loose and threatened to trip a Traveler on the stage. Seams ripped out after being stressed by acrobatic leaps. Glass jewels slipped their stitching, along with brilliantly dyed feathers and luxurious strips of fur.

Now I sat on the back steps of a wagon in the bright light of midday, flexing my fingers and blinking furiously to make my eyes focus on the fine work spread across my lap. I had spent the better part of the morning laboring over Patrius's cloak. It was a hideously complicated garment with row after row of colored feathers arrayed like a rainbow from the shoulders to the feet. It had taken me hours to stitch in the score of plumes that had come loose the night before, victims of a Traveler's overeager leap through a hidden trapdoor. I was secretly proud of the work I had completed; I could not tell my apprentice stitches from those of the master Travelers who had worked the garment many times before me.

Alas, my next project was giving me much more trouble. Caw offered up his criticism, cocking his head at an infuriating angle. *"That hem isn't flat."*

"I know," I said through gritted teeth. I had already ripped out my work twice; my stitches kept wandering in an uneven line.

*"Your sister Robina could make that hem lie flat. She could sew anything."*

"I know," I repeated. Despite Mother's most intense instruction back home, I had never been much good with detailed work.

*"Robina was the finest seamstress in your family."*

"Enough, Caw!" I shrugged hard, forcing him to take flight from my hunched shoulder. I rubbed at the padding sewn into my garment, trying to convey the notion that my poor stitchery was all his fault. He didn't notice, though. He'd settled on the eaves of the wagon, turning his back to me and fluffing his feathers as if he'd been struggling to fly against a brutal winter wind.

I couldn't say if Caw's words stung because they were criticism, or because he spoke of Robina in the past tense. I might have chosen to leave my family, but I didn't like to think of them as gone.

I caught my lip between my teeth and started to rip out the hem for the third time. My throat tightened as I remembered Robina on her wedding day, standing beside Lastor as they both were draped with the ladysilk flowers sacred to Madrina. Robina had been so happy—nearly as excited as when she had told Mother she was expecting a child. I'd left Silver Hollow only two weeks before, but I could already picture Robina growing heavy with her baby, with the treasured boy or girl I would never see.

Now my misery about Robina was heightened by a hefty dose

of guilt. I should not have chastised Caw—not when my dark-beast had only stated the truth. Not when he was only telling me what I already knew. Robina *could* fashion anything out of any type of cloth. All the women in Silver Hollow asked for her guid-ance when it came to tricky projects such as nameday garments or gowns for glorydays.

How many times had Robina shown me how to make even stitches? How many times had she demonstrated her technique for fashioning invisible seams? Certainly, she had been a hard taskmistress, but she'd always had my best interests at heart. She had always wanted to teach me, to train me, to make me a better girl so that some good man would eventually want me for his wife. She had wanted to make me be my best.

Just like Caw meant to do.

"Maybe you're right, Caw." I pitched my voice low so that no one would overhear me.

He replied so quickly that I knew he had been listening to my every move, even if he had kept his back to me. *"Of course I'm right. I'm always right."* He shifted and cocked his head at a jaunty angle. *"What was I right about this time?"*

"Robina. Silver Hollow. I never should have left home."

Caw made a chittering sound at the back of his throat. *"Ready to head back to your Mother, then? To your sisters? We can get halfway there before the Inquisitors find us."*

Of course. The Inquisitors. I was safe as long as I remained hidden among the Travelers. But if Caw and I set out on our own, we wouldn't last a week. Bony fingers of fear rattled around my heart as I imagined myself surrounded by snow-white robes. I sniffed hard and pressed my fingers beneath my eyes, dashing away sudden, hot tears.

My gesture was just in time. Vala bolted up the stairs of the wagon, throwing herself onto the step beside me. A startled Caw flung his wings wide, beating the air as he fought to keep his balance on the edge of the wagon's roof.

"Quick!" Vala said. Her beautiful black eyes were open wide. Her thick eyelashes batted against her cheeks as she threw a frantic glance over her shoulder. "Hide this!"

She shoved a shirt at me, one of the loose, homespun garments that the Traveler boys and men wore when they weren't in costumes. I took the thing without thinking, stashing it beneath Patrius's feathered cloak.

As I fumbled with the clothes, Vala grabbed at my next project, the mask of Aurelius. The god of wealth had lost half a dozen of the gold-painted coins that were supposed to be suspended from ribbons across his forehead. Vala grabbed for a spool of golden thread, measuring a length as if she'd spent all morning contemplating how to repair the mask.

I had barely finished tucking away the homespun sleeve when

Goran skidded around the corner of the wagon. "Give it back!" he demanded to Vala, ignoring me entirely.

"What?" If I hadn't known she was guilty—and if I hadn't seen her practice a dozen different emotions for her roles in the troupe's revels—I would have believed she had no idea what Goran was talking about.

"I know you took my extra shirt from Taggart's wagon. Give it back!"

"I haven't been anywhere near your grandfather's wagon." Vala turned Aurelius's mask, so that the coins that were still attached jangled softly. "See?" She waved a hand toward my mending and shot me a quick sideways glance. "Keara and I have been working all morning."

"Goran," I said, trying to force my voice into an annoyed register, even as I fought down my pleasure that Vala trusted me enough to fold me into her intrigue. "Could you take a step back? You're blocking my light."

He sighed in exasperation, but he moved away. Everyone in the troupe understood the importance of mending the costumes. Everyone knew the stage clothes must be kept in perfect order so that the revels could be performed without a hitch.

Vala twisted her wrist prettily, letting the sunlight glint off the gold paint on Aurelius's mask. "I'll help you find your shirt after I finish with these coins."

Goran set his hands on his hips. "You truly didn't take it?"

Vala met his eyes steadily. "I truly didn't take it."

I made a show of threading my needle, of bracing myself to begin working Mortana's hem one last time. Pretending I had the skill of a Traveler, I rolled my head as if I were easing a crick in my neck, and then I glanced toward the sun. "Isn't it time for you to get to the cook fires, Goran? Didn't Keon say he would need your help frying dumplings?"

Goran was assigned to help Keon, Vala's father, for the entire week. After that the responsibility would rotate; I was scheduled to serve for the next fortnight.

Goran hated laboring over the cook fires. I'd already heard Taggart tell him—twice—to take his petulance to his darkbeast. Somehow, though, Wart wasn't very adept at taking away Goran's faults. Actually, I couldn't imagine that midnight black toad absolving anyone of anything. All I had ever seen her do was sit in her cast-iron cage, pumping the bellows of her leathery throat and waiting for Goran to feed her crickets and worms.

Now the boy sighed like the weight of a thousand wooden stages were strapped to his shoulders. With one final glare at Vala, he disappeared around the corner of the wagon. I barely waited for him to get out of earshot before I whispered to Vala, "Why did you take his shirt?"

"Quick," she said. "Give it to me."

I retrieved the garment and passed it across. Vala put aside Aurelius's mask so that she could dig deep in the pocket of her skirt. She moved quickly, confidently, as if she lied to Goran every single day of her life. Which, I speculated, she probably did. She wasted no time unwrapping a crumpled scrap of linen.

I peered at the dusty remains of a dried plant. A cluster of white hooks snagged the cloth. "Sow thistle! What are you doing with that?"

"Hush!" She touched the collar of Goran's shirt to the gray-green debris.

"Vala," I warned. "He'll itch for days!"

She completed her ministrations with efficient gestures, rubbing in the last of the sow thistle before carefully folding and stowing away her kerchief. "It'll serve him right," she said evenly.

"What did Goran do to you?" I was afraid of the answer, afraid of the terrible things Vala would say. I glanced at Caw, to see if he had some wisdom to share. My darkbeast, though, was ignoring me. His onyx gaze was directed at Vala, as if he were eager to hear her retort.

She did not disappoint. "In Clementius's name, what *hasn't* he done?" Vala brushed her fingers over her wrist. I had already learned that the gesture meant she was thinking of her own darkbeast, of Slither's customary morning warming spot. Clearly, Vala's struggles with Goran had sent her to her darkbeast in the past.

More times than she cared to remember, by the grim set of her jaw. "He put a common garter snake in Slither's basket one morning, hiding my darkbeast until well past noon. He dusted my hair with flour while I slept. He dosed my silberry tea with rabbitgrass so that my teeth turned green, the very night that I was to perform in *Clementius and the Mariner.* And just the night before you joined us, he sewed shut the arms of my spare blouses, both of them."

She drew herself up straighter with the recitation of each of Goran's crimes. I knew Vala was a Traveler; I understood she was weaving a story for my entertainment. But I couldn't help being carried along by her indignation. I couldn't help but be swayed by her wounded pride. She leaned close and whispered conspiratorially, "And that's just what he's done since the Flower Moon!"

I glanced at Goran's innocent-appearing shirt. "It was only a little sow thistle," I finally said. Caw shifted on the wagon above me.

"Not much at all," Vala agreed.

"And if the itch is truly bad, he can always find some spider balm." Caw craned his neck as I spoke, as if he were looking for someone, for a good girl, a truthful child.

"I saw a stand of it myself, yesterday, not far from the riverbank," Vala affirmed.

I was captured by the earnest expression on her face. Her exotic curls were swept up in a brilliant crimson ribbon, so that they tumbled around her shoulders, turning her into some fantastic noblewoman. Her lips were pursed just a little, and she held her breath, waiting for me to make up my mind, to decide whether or not to betray her. Her eyes held mine, steady and unblinking.

"Very well," I said at last, taking care not to catch even a glimpse of Caw out of the corner of my eye. "I won't say anything to Goran."

Vala's smile was brighter than the sun beating down upon us. "Thank you, Keara-ti! I knew you'd understand!"

The endearment tripped off her tongue as if we'd been sisters all our lives. I was thrilled by the way she said my child-name, trusting, *loving*. My heart pounded, as if I'd just won a footrace. To cover the sound, I laughed, long and loud. "Vala-ti," I said. "Just don't let your father find out."

She grinned. "He'd only make me offer up my rebellion to Slither. Now, are you going to help me sneak this shirt back into Taggart's wagon?"

I laughed and picked up the feathered cape for Patrius. "I suppose it *is* time for me to return this costume to its proper place."

"Blessed Patrius!" Vala exclaimed. "Answer to all our prayers!" We both knew Taggart's wagon housed all the costumes for the father of all the gods. It should be simple, replacing Goran's shirt at the same time we returned the feathered cloak.

Caw flapped his wings, obviously intending to take his perch on my shoulder. I draped the cape over Caw's padding, though. I did not want to hear what my darkbeast would say about my game with Vala. Not that he could truly chastise me. After all, I had not offered up my action, had not brought my mischief to him in any formal way.

"Ach," Vala said, waving her hand above her head to keep Caw from landing on her. "What does that wretched animal want?"

Wretched Caw. I was supposed to despise him. I was supposed to resent every moment I spent with him. "I don't know," I said in an offhand tone that would have made any Traveler proud. "But if he isn't careful, he'll be picking sow thistle from his feathers."

"*You wouldn't!*" Caw challenged, circling higher in the air above us.

"*Stay out of this, Caw.*"

"*Whatever you command,* Keara-ti." I heard the sharp emphasis Caw placed on my child-name; he was mocking me for yielding to Vala. I chose to ignore him, though. To pretend that he had not spoken. That he was not right.

Caw veered into the woods, croaking a noisy protest. As Vala and I picked up our pace, Keon began ringing the brass bell, summoning the troupe to the midday meal. My belly growled at the thought of the fried dumplings that had so conveniently spirited Goran away.

I would save one for Caw. He would forgive me after I gave him a treat.

# Chapter Ten

Another week on the Great Road. Another two villages. Chance after chance for me to fall further in love with my new life.

Goran wore his spare shirt, and he suffered a rash of itchy bubbles where the collar touched his flesh. At first Vala pretended innocence, but ultimately she confessed. Keon told her to take her cruelty to Slither while I found some spider balm for Goran. No adult ordered me to take my own actions to my darkbeast. No one needed to—Caw watched over me with condemning eyes.

In less time than I would have expected, though, the incident was forgotten. Half a dozen more pranks had played out between Vala and Goran by the time we arrived at Rivermeet.

Fifty Silver Hollows could have melted into the streets of that town. Pastures lined the Great Road long before we arrived, their neat diagonal fences holding cows separate from sheep separate from goats. Crops thrived in the neatly plowed fields; the rich, dark earth was hidden by the burgeoning harvest. Arriving from the south, we passed Pondera's round wooden godhouse.

"Caw," I whispered, trying to take in the size of the structure. A hundred trees must have been cut down to build it—big ones, from the heart of the forest.

*"She's still the same goddess of balance,"* Caw said, his voice nonchalant. *"She still welcomes travelers, with soft beds and good food. Go inside the godhouse! Let's check Pondera's food!"*

We did not honor Pondera, though. Instead we continued into Rivermeet. The town was wealthy enough to have structures for all the gods.

Caw huddled closer as we passed an open-roofed square structure. Men were inside—many of them—for I heard their voices raised in lusty shouts. The cries were drowned out by the clang of metal on metal, and I realized we were passing a site dedicated to Marius, the god of war.

Madrina's stone circle was next, set back from the road in a swath of emerald grass. A half dozen cows eyed us placidly, living embodiments of the sigil for the mother of all the gods. One beast lowed softly as her calf started to nuzzle for milk.

Mortana's rectangle of stacked slate followed, the individual stones looking precarious. The goddess of death always made me nervous, even when I wasn't arriving at the largest town I had ever seen. As if he were aware of my anxiety, Caw fluttered up to Mortana's gate, perching on the stone lintel. He folded his wings precisely, turning himself into a mirror image of Mortana's white raven sigil.

"Caw! Come down from there!"

*"You should see the view,"* he said. *"They have godhouses for every one of the Twelve."*

I snapped my fingers and glanced around at the Travelers. It would not do for them to think that Caw was mocking Mortana.

*"Do you think I should stay here?"* he asked. *"Don't we make a lovely pair?"*

"Now!" I commanded.

*"What do you think Mortana's raven eats?"*

"Bare bones and slimy water. And that's all that you'll get if you don't come to me right now."

I don't know if it was the threat of starvation or fear of being left behind, but Caw finally abandoned his perch. I had never been so grateful for the feel of him settling on my shoulder. His presence was a comfort, a familiarity in the midst of so much that was strange.

It was almost enough to make me forget to look at Patrius's

godhouse as our carts rumbled past. Almost. But not quite. And the sight that greeted my eyes made my breath catch in my throat.

An Inquisitor was framed in the marble doorway. The man's white robe glinted as if it were made of the same hard stone. He stood perfectly still, but I could imagine his chains rattling as we passed. I shivered at the unheard whisper of his knife easing from the sheath slung around his waist. I wondered how many Lost roamed the streets of a town as large as Rivermeet.

"*All is well,*" Caw crooned inside my head. "*No one is paying attention to you. Not with all the Travelers surrounding you. Don't worry, Keara-ti. All is well.*"

And Caw was right. The Inquisitor made no move toward our little procession.

In short order we found the market square. Rivermeet was too big to have a green. Instead the Travelers would be required to pay for the privilege of setting up their wagons in the common market—a full tithe of all the earnings from the revels they performed. Those coins would be passed on to the merchants they displaced.

Taggart had already warned us as we passed the edge of town—we could not sleep in the open air that night. We must all crowd into the wagons, protecting the Travelers' property even as we kept ourselves safe from the inevitable Rivermeet rogues. We would watch over the stage closely, make sure that the clever wooden structure remained unharmed by the curious, the playful, or the malicious.

Keon quickly claimed a space for his cook fire, a circle well sheltered by the wagons. We children had collected a great deal of wood the previous two nights, filling the undercarriage of every wagon so that we would not run out while we stayed in the town. Even so, Vala's father had vowed to offer more cold foods than usual, drawing especially on the goat's milk cheese that Rivermeet had made famous, even in distant Austeria. I was eager to see what he would provide.

Vala was not as interested in her father's cooking plans as I was. In fact, she lost no time getting to work with her own valuable mission. She was determined to cry the show, to bring in the largest crowds we had yet seen on the Great Road. And I was going to help her, at least until Keon required my services late that afternoon.

I threw back my shoulders in anticipation. Caw grumbled his dissatisfaction with my sudden movement, and I clicked my tongue to tell him to settle down.

"You're not going to take that thing, are you?" Vala's nose turned up as if she smelled something rotten.

I started to protest, but I stopped myself just in time. A normal child would not want to be followed by her darkbeast. A normal child would be grateful for an afternoon of freedom. "Stay here, you," I said roughly.

I wanted to take back the command when Caw fluttered to the most distant wagon.

Vala guided me through the streets. We picked our way to a pretty fountain where a dozen women waited to collect water for the day. Vala showed me how to stand at the edge of the square, how to push back my shoulders and throw out my arms so that I seemed to take up more space than any one girl could really occupy. She demonstrated a way to summon my breath from the pit of my belly. She instructed me to pitch my voice low, to pour strength into my words so they could be heard from all the way across the square. She taught me what to say as well, how to string together rhymes, one word after another. All this so that the townsfolk would remember my chant until the Travelers began to perform their actual revels, two days hence. Two days, to build anticipation. Two days, to reap the largest harvest of copper coins and—if we were lucky—silver.

At the first square I merely watched Vala. At the second I stood beside her. At the third I raised my voice, crying with her to convince people to join us for the revels.

I had an advantage, there in Rivermeet. I recognized the people. I knew who each of them was.

Oh, I didn't actually know the townsfolk. I had never set foot in Rivermeet before.

But I recognized a clutch of shepherds' wives from the yellow stains on their hands, the permanent reminder of the wool fat they handled every day. I found an herb woman by the tang of marrin berries, the tiny blue fruits of late summer that needed to be roasted before the new moon leached away all their healing powers. I discovered four generations of one family, all gossiping together, recognizable from the snatches of the Family Rule they bandied about as they spoke.

Each time I identified someone, I whispered my realization to Vala. She scarcely nodded, but she wove the information into her patter, folding it into her rhymes as if she'd known about the specific townsfolk all along. Her revised words carried additional weight, drew people in more and more completely. Each listener came to believe that the Travelers carried a direct appeal, a personal message.

I made the Travelers' magic real.

I could barely contain my excitement as I helped Keon prepare supper. He had procured great baskets of early-harvest pears; he said they went especially well with the tangy goat cheese. There were flatbreads, too, cooked over the smallest of fires, and a bowl of mixed pickles made from the finest vegetables Keon had found in the marketplace. In my role as cooking assistant, I ate last, but plenty of food remained.

That night Taggart walked from wagon to wagon, listening to the Travelers describe their days. Vala stood like a soldier to make her report. "We found three new mothers getting water from the Doll's Fountain. All gave birth to boys."

Taggart nodded. "We'll work the children into one of the Common Plays."

"The crops have grown well, and the remaining harvest is expected to be good," Vala went on. "Every man, woman, and child had a tax tattoo."

Another nod from Taggart. "More coins for all of us," he rumbled.

"At least eight children had blackwater fever in the past fortnight. All from Eastmill, across the Floating Bridge. We heard of no special offerings to Mortana, though, so all must have lived."

Taggart's bushy eyebrows met above the stone line of his nose. "And how do you know they fell ill in the first place?"

"They smelled of dead man's hand." Vala's response was so perfect, so confident, that I almost believed she had recognized the stink of the seedpods on her own. I almost believed that she hadn't stolen the knowledge from me, that she wasn't parroting back the very words I had spoken to her while we cried the revel in the settlement on the far side of the Silver.

Taggart nodded as he rested a hand on Vala's head, spreading his fingers wide. He looked like Patrius's own priest bestowing a blessing. "Very good, child. You serve your troupe well." He reached deep in his pocket, and I was astonished to see him produce a copper coin. "And now the troupe will serve you."

Late that night I sat on the edge of the Travelers' marketplace camp, huddling in the doorway of a shuttered shop as I nursed a grudge. Caw was perched on the window frame beside me. "It's not fair," I whispered for the hundredth time. "I should have gotten that coin."

*"All is fair on the Travelers' road."*

"But Vala used the things I told her. Taggart thinks that she's the one who sees things, that she's the one who knows. *I'm* the one who told her about the dead man's hand. She wouldn't have recognized that stench without me."

*"What difference does it make? A good harvest fills all bellies. Speaking of which?"*

Keon had finished the feast with apple biscuits. I had eaten one but saved the rest of my portion for Caw, knowing he would appreciate the honeyed sweetness. I produced the treat from my pocket, even as I muttered, "Taggart should have thanked *me*. He should have said that *I* served the troupe well."

*"Shall we go to him now so that you can plead your case?"*

I glared at my darkbeast. He knew me best in all the world, and yet he was mocking me. He knew I would never challenge Vala openly. Not when I needed the Travelers. Not when I needed the troupe to let me stay, to travel with them when they left Rivermeet.

Caw ruffled his feathers and swallowed the last of my apple biscuit. He shuddered, from the crest of his head to the end of his tail feathers, as if he were overwhelmed by the luxury of the treat. *"Perhaps Taggart has a few apple biscuits of his own? Ones he wants to give away? We could chat with him, just to find out."*

Certainly. I was going to knock on the door of Taggart's wagon. I would tell Goran I just wanted to chat with his grandfather for a moment or two, just long enough to see if he had any extra sweets for my obnoxious raven darkbeast. And oh, by the way, the Travelers should be grateful enough to me for my crying the show that they should let me stay on after Rivermeet, travel with them all the way to the cath in Lutecia.

I sighed and grumbled, "No more apple biscuits for you. Let's go." I barely stifled a yawn as I gathered him up, as I climbed into the wagon that was my home for as long as we stayed in Rivermeet. It was close inside, with a dozen bodies huddled on the wooden floor, all sleeping soundly.

Caw fluttered to a perch on the darkened lantern that hung from the center post, and I picked my way through the crowd. As I lowered myself beside Vala, she rolled over and offered me half of her blanket. She mumbled something that sounded like "Coughing thread."

"What?" I whispered, poking her shoulder to make her wake up a little more.

"In the morning." She was almost asleep again before she said, "Toffee bread."

She started to snore softly. I turned onto my side and stared up at Caw, but there was nothing more to say. My darkbeast gazed at me long into the night, his unblinking eyes barely visible in the gloom.

Vala woke before me, tugging me out of the wagon before I was fully awake. "Come on," she whispered as I looked around the barely stirring market. "We want to get there while it's still hot."

"Get where? While what's still hot?" My thoughts were still fogged with a tangled dream about Bestius and Inquisitors and the midnight rainbow of Caw's wings. I remembered my obligation to Keon, and I said, "I can't go anywhere. I need to help your father."

"We'll be back in plenty of time."

"Vala—"

"Fine," she said, tugging at my hand. "I'll help you when we get back. With four hands it will be as if we were not gone at all."

Before I could continue my protest, before I could even think to find Caw, Vala trotted away from the Travelers' wagons. I shrugged and followed her down a series of side streets, each one narrower than the last. We made three turns, and I thought we might be near the Doll's Fountain from the day before. Before I could ask, though, Vala ducked into a dark alley, glancing over her shoulder with a laughing command for me to hurry.

And then I smelled it. Hot. Yeasty. The golden scent of fresh-baked bread.

My belly rumbled as if I had not eaten since Silver Hollow. Vala laughed again and said, "Come on, then!" She dragged me through a nearby doorway.

I could not believe my eyes. We stood in a shop filled with wooden shelves that stretched from floor to ceiling. Great loaves of bread were stacked high, as if an army were expected to march through for provisions. There were rounds of chestnut bread, huge pillows of crusty wheat—more than Silver Hollow would ever bake for a dozen nameday celebrations. Some of the loaves were studded with cheese, and others were decorated with slices of apple. A giantess stood behind a counter, watching over a linen-covered basket, her bare arms flushed red across her chest.

"Good day, Mistress Baker," Vala said, dropping a sweet curtsy for the woman.

"Recolta bless us all," the baker replied. Of course she'd be partial to the goddess of the harvest. Without Recolta's protection she'd lack any wares to sell.

Vala fished Taggart's copper coin out of a hidden pocket. "Three toffee breads, if you please." She set the coin on the counter. A beam of early sunlight had followed us through the doorway, and Vala made sure the copper glinted like gold before she surrendered it.

The baker folded back the linen from her basket. Inside there was a clutch of loaves, each half as big as my head. The woman took her time selecting three for Vala, scrutinizing each round as if it were the most important sale she had ever made.

Vala accepted the bread with the same gravity, ducking her chin as she received each one. She slipped the treasures into a woolen sack that she had produced from somewhere in the swirl of her skirts. "Many thanks," she said. "Come see the Travelers in the market tomorrow night, goodwife. We'll play a piece for Recolta."

The woman's eyes narrowed. "I may do that. Yes, I may."

I followed Vala out the door. She picked her way through the streets of Rivermeet as if she'd lived there her entire life. I wondered how often she had come to this town, when the Travelers had last passed through. I felt a curious twist of envy that all the people we passed had seen the Travelers more than I had ever been able to do, back in Silver Hollow.

At the market the merchants were in full cry, touting fresh wares that had just come in from the Great Road. Early apples were laid out in pyramids, and golden honey glinted in pots. One vendor had great lengths of cloth, woven from the past spring's shearing. A cooper's young apprentice hawked buckets, and another child boasted that he had the finest twig brooms for sale.

We passed them all, ducking behind the largest of the Travelers' wagons as if we were passing through our own city's gates. Keon looked up from the cook fire, an unspoken command in eyes as dark as Vala's. I started to dart over to his side, but my attention was snagged by Goran. The boy was just descending Taggart's stairs, rubbing sleep from his eyes.

Vala opened her sack as he stumbled forward. "For us," she said without ceremony. "Toffee bread," she clarified, but then she slapped Goran's hand as he grabbed the largest of the loaves. "That belongs to Keara-ti. She was the one who cried our revels. She told Taggart about blackwater fever, about the grateful audience we can expect, and she was the one to receive his reward."

My jaw dropped as I stared at her. I had not told Taggart anything at all; Vala had. She shrugged away my astonishment, though, as if to say it was all the same once the grain was ground. I felt shy as I accepted the largest loaf.

I shouldn't have despaired to Caw the night before. I shouldn't have complained about Vala. I wondered if my darkbeast had understood Vala's generosity all along, if he had known she would repay me in this utterly unexpected way. I would have to save Caw a bite or two of toffee bread, to make up for my complaints.

Goran grumbled at Vala's rebuke, but he accepted the slightly smaller loaf. Vala nodded at me, as if to say that I should go first. Carefully I tore my bread into two equal pieces. Steam rose up from the soft white clouds of baked dough. Nuggets of toffee melted through each half, fragrant with rich, sweetened butter. All three of us laughed, and I sank my teeth into the treasure.

Sweet warmth flooded my mouth, and I closed my eyes in rapture. "Thank you," I mumbled around a mouthful of bread. "Vala, this is amazing!"

Silence. Vala did not respond to my words. Goran, either. I opened my eyes, wondering if they were so intent on gulping their own bread that they could not spare a single sound. But neither Vala nor Goran was gulping. Instead, both of them stared at me, their faces ashen, their eyes bulging in horror.

No.

They weren't staring at me. They were looking *behind* me, above me, at something over my right shoulder.

Before I could turn around, a low voice hissed, "Blessings of all the gods on you, heretic beast. What sort of child are you, not to offer up thanks to the Twelve before you eat?"

I whirled around to face an Inquisitor's snow-white robe.

# Chapter Eleven

I couldn't see the Inquisitor's face; it was lost inside his pointed white hood. I could see his hands, though, his long bony fingers, traced with snakes of blue green veins. Those claws clamped down on my shoulders. A strangled cry broke from my lips, the wordless sound of all my nightmares waking me at once.

In the midst of my panic I thought to find Caw. He would know what to do. He could tell me what to say. But my darkbeast was still in the Travelers' wagon where I had left him when Vala led me out to the bakery. I scrambled to collect my thoughts, to reach out to Caw with my mind.

My heart was pounding too hard, though; I could not hear *myself* think, much less channel silent communication to an unseen raven. My terror tripled as I realized I would never get a chance to say good-bye to my darkbeast. I would never have a chance to offer up my final failings, to say all the things I should have said in the long years that he had been my companion.

My friend.

The Inquisitor's hands tightened, forcing me to take a step closer. His hood shifted, as if he were tilting his head, and I could imagine his eyes boring into me, burning a path deep into my memories. Could he somehow tell that I was a child who had failed to kill her darkbeast? Did he know that I belonged in Silver Hollow, not in Rivermeet? Had he realized that I was Lost?

"Yes," he hissed, as if he *could* read my mind. "Patrius's god-house could use a heretic like you. Patrius will guide you on the righteous paths of all the Twelve."

I realized then that a stag was embroidered above his heart, the snow-white threads nearly invisible against the shimmering fabric of his gown. The animal's antlers branched elaborately, each ending in a dozen sharpened points. This Inquisitor was specially pledged to the father of all the gods, then.

At least he wasn't sworn to Bestius. Praise the Twelve for some small mercy.

I needed to say something, do something, make use of all the skills Vala had taught me the day before. If I could harness the Travelers' way of speaking, of making people believe what I wanted them to believe, I still might escape from the Inquisitor's grasp. To my horror, though, my voice remained frozen inside my throat.

*My* voice was frozen, but not everyone's. "Hold!" The command rang out, sharp and clear. The Inquisitor's fingers tightened even more, burning into my shoulders like the embers at the heart of Keon's cook fire. In my dazed state it took me a moment to realize that the cry had come from the largest of the Travelers' wagons. "Stand down, honored lord!"

I craned my neck to see Taggart framed on the top step of his wagon, looking like Patrius himself. The old Traveler's ornate iron necklace tangled across his chest like a living thing, commanding almost as much attention as his stentorian voice. He raised both hands as if to emphasize his words, and he suddenly seemed larger than the very buildings that surrounded the market square.

I realized then that the Inquisitor and I marked the center of a circle. We were surrounded by all the Travelers. A few merchants had sussed out the commotion as well; they ringed the troupe. Townsfolk gaped at the very outer limit of the circle, suddenly more interested in witnessing an Inquisitor's wrath than in finding the best bargains at the market.

I felt like I was standing on the Travelers' stage, like I was the lead performer in some new revel.

At Taggart's cry the Inquisitor's hands loosened on my shoulders, but he did not set me free. I managed to turn sideways, to face Taggart on his majestic stairway. Any hope of gaining freedom, though, was dashed when the Inquisitor intoned, "This Lost one must learn to love the gods. She must come to Patrius's godhouse."

"She's a troublesome child," Taggart agreed, sounding as if my chronic disobedience had exhausted him. "But she is not the true problem." He pointed his finger, like Venerius shooting his golden shaft, and I was shocked to realize he was directing everyone's attention to Goran, to his own grandson. "If you're searching for the root of mischief in this camp, that's the one you want to take."

I gasped in horror. How could the Travelers be so cold? How could they direct the Inquisitor's wrath at an innocent boy?

As if on cue, Goran took a stumbling step forward, and I barely caught his strangled whisper: "Grandfather!"

Taggart ignored his own flesh and blood, speaking directly to the Inquisitor. "If you want the leader of all the Travelers' imps, that's the one. He forgets the Twelve, no matter how often *I* remind him. He avoids prayer like ordinary boys avoid soap. If you can teach that one about Patrius, you'll have truly honored the gods."

The Inquisitor's voice was iron as he shook my shoulders, rattling my teeth and nearly making me bite my own tongue. "But this one is so Lost that she yields to *his* wrongdoing. I'll take both children and try to guide them both back to the ways of the Twelve."

Taggart scoffed. "It will do no good, I tell you. The girl doesn't have the wits of a plucked pigeon."

The criticism stung, and I started to protest. Vala, though, chose that moment to clench her fingers into a fist. The motion drew my attention, and I saw the way she turned her foot . . . just . . . so. She tilted her head at a slight angle. Sure enough, the actions made her look simple, as if she could not quite be trusted to count to ten without losing a number or two.

I swallowed my angry words and did my best to imitate her. Relaxing my gaze, I let my attention be snagged by the pennants that snapped on the very edge of the market square.

Taggart didn't spare me a glance, though, no matter how well I imitated Vala. Instead he laded all of his attention on Goran. "We Travelers would be grateful if you could do anything to bring that boy in line. Take him for a day, teach him respect for the gods, and for his elders, too. Of course, we would pay you for such a difficult labor." As if he had planned on offering a bribe all along, the old Traveler plunged a hand into the folds of his robe.

The Inquisitor finally withdrew his grasp from my shoulders. My flesh throbbed where his fingers had dug in, and I was certain I would have bruises by noon. For now, though, I was captivated by the scene before me: Taggart, counting a few copper coins into the Inquisitor's suddenly cupped palm.

The robed man, though, did not move when the counting was

complete. Taggart's eyes narrowed, and he produced a silver coin, adding its cool sparkle to the honeyed copper.

Still the Inquisitor stood motionless.

Another silver coin. Another. Twelve silver coins in all before the counting was through. One for each of the gods.

And finally the Inquisitor pocketed the wealth. "Fine," he said, his voice as cold as iron chains. He nudged Goran with a leather-clad toe. "Come, Lost boy. It is time to learn the ways of Patrius."

Goran scrambled to his feet and danced a few steps away, obviously trying to avoid further acquaintance with the Inquisitor's brutal boot. I caught the glance that Goran shot my way, the jagged shock written plainly across his face. Before he could say anything, before I could try to save him from the fate that should have been mine, the Inquisitor clasped his arm and bullied him out of the marketplace.

The crowd had not yet closed around them when Vala dragged me up the steps of the nearest wagon. She closed the door behind us, as if she feared the Inquisitor would look back, would change his mind. Stunned by what I had just witnessed, by how close I had come to being taken, I barely registered that this was the refuge where we had bedded down for the night.

My darkbeast fluttered down from the lantern, taking his customary place on my shoulder. Out of the corner of my eye I could see him turning his head this way and that, as if he did not recognize me, as if he did not understand how I could have let another serve the sentence I deserved.

"Twelve silver coins," Vala gasped.

"We have to go after him!"

"Twelve," she repeated, still clearly shocked.

"Now, Vala-ti. Before it's too late. Before the Inquisitor—"

She interrupted me, as if I hadn't said a thing. "I don't believe it. We've never paid more than six."

"Never?" The word cut through my panic. "You mean, the Inquisitors have come before?"

She rolled her onyx eyes. "The Inquisitors *always* take their cut."

My knees started to tremble violently, and I almost upset Caw from my shoulder as I collapsed onto one of the wagon's bolted chairs. The Inquisitors always came to the Travelers. This one had not come because he suspected me. He had not come because of Caw. Our secret was still safe.

But Goran had been taken. And Taggart had let him go—had *argued* for him to go. "I don't understand," I moaned. "Why did Taggart do it? Why did he pay twice as much to send off Goran instead of me?"

"Twice?" Vala looked as confused as I felt. She shook her head, and her voice dropped to a whisper. "Keara-ti, Taggart paid twelve *silvers*. We never pay more than half a dozen copper coins. Ever."

Before I could even begin to figure out the meaning behind

those words, the wagon door crashed open. Taggart stormed in, his embroidered robes swirling around him like a thunderhead. "Out!" he shouted to Vala. She squeaked and darted through the door, pulling it closed before Taggart finished bellowing, "You've cost me, girl!"

"My lord?"

He snorted in irritation. "I'm not your lord. Don't flatter me with titles."

"Taggart," I said carefully, squirming beneath his glare. "If you please, my—Taggart." I couldn't think of an explanation, of a single reason why the Travelers would have paid so much, only to lose Goran. Only to lose their own instead of me. Instead of a rank outsider. "Why?" I finally managed to ask.

Taggart grimaced. "No one wants an Inquisitor poking around their camp, do they?" For a single heartbeat he flashed a glance at Caw, and I feared he knew the entire truth about my darkbeast, about my twelfth nameday come and gone. But that was utterly impossible. There was no way Taggart could know my hidden past. "Do they?" Taggart repeated, the two words as loud as a smith banging on his anvil.

"No," I whispered.

"You've never been seized by an Inquisitor before. You don't know how they work. The man would have asked you questions, girl, demanded answers that would have put us all at risk."

"Risk?" I couldn't help but squeak the question.

Taggart made a dismissive sound. "I've listened to Vala filling your mind in the nighttime, under the stars, when she thought no one was close enough to hear. I know she's told you about our plans for the cath."

The *cath*? What did the cath have to do with anything? I nodded, though, because I had to do something, had to respond to Taggart's accusation.

"If I paid twelve silvers to get that fool Inquisitor *out* of our camp, you can be certain another troupe paid nearly as much to get him in. Don't look so shocked, girl—it's been done before! That's why we lost the cath two years back, because another company stole our costume designs. They bought off the Inquisitors in Cooper Falls, had them go through every one of our wagons. They mimicked every mask, every sigil, and we ended up looking like poor pretenders, instead of the troupe with new ideas."

Fine. I understood now why Taggart had paid, why he had spent so much to make the Inquisitor leave. But that didn't explain everything. That didn't tell me why the old man had condemned his own grandson in my place. "You didn't need to sacrifice Goran! I could have kept a secret!"

"Could you?" He pounded both hands on the table in front of me, making Caw grip my bruised shoulder even tighter. Taggart leaned close enough that his necklace seemed to shimmer, and I squeezed my eyes closed, turning my face away. "Could you keep a secret from a holy Inquisitor, Keara? One intent on learning everything you have to hide?" When I did not answer, he snorted his disgust. "I had no choice but to send Goran in your stead."

Molten tears scalded my cheeks, and I whispered, "I'm sorry."

"Sorry doesn't fill our coffers." Taggart's tone stung more than hornmoon on a fresh cut. "With twelve silvers gone, we *have* to win the cath. We'll never meet the titheman's new year tally otherwise. We'll have no way to get the whole troupe back together in Austeria."

"I'll repay you," I croaked, my voice as raw as Caw's.

"With what?" I realized immediately that I had been wrong. *I* was not the one who sounded like Caw. Taggart did. His voice was hoarse. Harsh. Disbelieving. "I'll tell you what you'll do, girl. You'll work with us Travelers, from here to Lutecia. You'll help with whatever needs helping, you'll give whatever needs giving. Twelve silvers' worth of labor by the Hunter's Moon, and not a day before."

His demand was impossible. I could never work enough to pay back twelve silver coins, not in nine short weeks. But I had to answer, and so I said, "Yes, Taggart," in my best, most respectful whisper.

Even as I said the words, I had to tamp down a wild flicker of glee. Taggart did not know—he could *never* know—but he was granting my dearest dream. He was ordering me to stay with the Travelers all the way to the Primate's golden city. All the way to Lutecia.

He harrumphed and headed for the door.

"But, Taggart?" I asked, because I was never any good at letting vines grow where they twisted. He paused, but he did not turn around. "Goran. How can I save him? How can I get him back from the Inquisitor?"

To my astonishment, the old man laughed. Harsh and low, but laughter all the same. "What do they teach you in a place like Silver Hollow?" I had no idea how to answer that question. "Goran will be back by sunset. He'll be tired, and his hands will be rough from polishing Patrius's altar, but he'll be with us before dark."

I was stunned. "What? Tonight? That's all the Inquisitor . . . I—I don't know what to say!"

Taggart slid his gaze toward Caw. "You'll figure out something, I'm sure. Take it to your darkbeast."

I was still gaping as he left the wagon. Taggart had known all along that Goran's punishment would be complete in a day. Vala had too. Here I'd been thinking I had condemned Goran to a short and brutal life of torture, to horrible destruction at the hands of Patrius's Inquisitor. No one—not a single person—had thought to set me straight.

I started to laugh and cry at the same time. "I didn't understand," I said over and over again. Caw hopped from my shoulder to the table, turning his head first one way, then the other. "I didn't understand."

*"Are you going to keep saying that? I'll listen, of course, if that's what you really want. But it would be easier for me to pay attention if I wasn't starving."*

I was astonished to realize that somehow, impossibly, I had stashed my toffee bread in the pocket of my skirt. I must have stowed it away when the Inquisitor first appeared, before he clapped his hands onto my shoulders. Unable to imagine swallowing any of the treat after all that had happened, I broke up the bread for Caw. He downed a dozen generous bites—one for every silver coin Taggart had paid.

Finally I trusted my voice enough to say, "Caw, did you hear Taggart? He is *ordering* us to stay with him until Lutecia."

*"You worked that quite well. I hope Goran doesn't mind toiling for your passage today."*

"I didn't mean to hurt him, Caw!"

Caw ruffled his feathers. *"You could have spoken out."*

"It all happened so fast. Taggart didn't give me a chance to say or do anything."

Somehow Caw shrugged. *"Taggart did what he thought best. Adults do that sometimes."*

I thought about that. Taggart made decisions. Mother had

made decisions. Sometimes I wasn't very good at understanding the why and the wherefore of the people around me—even when they acted in my own best interest. "Caw," I said at last. "I don't know what I'm supposed to say. I don't even know what I'm supposed to be taking to you, what I'm supposed to offer up."

My darkbeast tilted his head, as if he were giving the matter great thought. After a long pause he said at last, *"I'll take your toffee bread. Forget it. It is mine."*

I snorted as I handed over the last bite. Somehow I'd have to earn a spare copper so that I could buy Goran a new loaf once he returned from Patrius's godhouse.

PART THREE

# Jealousy

*I was ten years old. Silver Hollow was celebrating Patrius's gloryday with a special feast, marking three hundred years that our cottages had stood beside the Silver River. A bull had been slaughtered in the god's honor, and the beef was spitted and cooked for everyone in the village. Musicians had been hired from three villages away, and the communal oven had been filled with baking bread for an entire week.*

*And then Mother told me I must stay in our cottage. By pure bad luck, the feast coincided with the anniversary of the day Father had died, two years before. Someone must be home, Mother said, in case Father's spirit came looking for us. We could not let him be lonely. We could not let him think we had forgotten him.*

*"It's not fair!" I cried, thinking of the meat juices dripping into the fire. "Why can't Robina stay behind?"*

"Robina hopes to dance with Lastor." Lastor. The blacksmith's apprentice. He had shoulders as broad as the bull we had sacrificed, and hands as sinewy as Father's grapevines.

"I want to dance with Lastor too," I said to Mother. "Let Morva stay here. I deserve to dance, just like Robina."

"You're a jealous, jealous girl," Mother said, and her mouth straightened into an angry line. "Take that to your darkbeast."

The rag leash hung loose beside Caw's cage. I stared after my mother and sisters as they left our home, and I listened to the strains of merriment from the green.

"May I have the honor of this dance?"

"Leave me alone, Caw."

"Robina has lived in the Women's Hall for four years already. She fears she will never find a husband. Let her dance with Lastor."

"But I love him!"

"You are ten years old. You don't know the meaning of the word 'love.' You are jealous."

"I am not." I closed my eyes, trying to picture Lastor's face. He had greeted me three months before, when Mother sent me down to the forge to collect an iron poker for our hearth. Now I lifted that tool and shifted its weight in my untethered hand. Idly I swept it back toward the fire, catching Mother's rat on the mantel. The stuffed darkbeast teetered on the wooden shelf, and I cried out, stretching to retrieve it before it hit *the hearth. Leashed, though, I could not reach it in time. The creature's whiskers were singed before I could dig it out of the fire.*

*Caw waited until I had returned the darkbeast to its place before he said,* "You only want to dance with Lastor because your sister does."

"That's not true!" *I brushed at Mother's rat, trying to clean it.* "I love him!"

"What color are his eyes?"

*They were brown, weren't they? Or were they green?*

"You want to be the one fussed over. You want to plan your wedding, even though you are only a girl. You want to be the wife of the blacksmith, but you don't care at all about Lastor."

*I had been thinking about the fine gown I would wear on my wedding day, the cloth of gold that would cover my hair, just as my mother had covered hers, and her mother before her. I had imagined people referring to me as Goodwife Smith, ducking their heads in recognition of all the power and prestige that I had in the village.* "Is there anything wrong with that?"

"You know Robina wants Lastor more. She baked the plum cake he likes, to give to him tonight."

*"Her cakes are too dry. He'll have to drink a flask of wine to choke down a slice," I muttered under my breath, but Caw heard me perfectly.*

"He'll know it is dry, and he'll finish every crumb."

*I waited for a long time, unwilling to admit that Caw was right.*

*That I was wrong. But when I really thought about it, I knew I didn't want to marry Lastor. I'd be happier roaming the fields, collecting the ladysilk flowers that would be woven into a cape, a garment large enough to cover the bride and groom on their wedding day.*

*"Fine," I said at last. "I hope Lastor asks Robina for every dance tonight."*

*Caw bobbed his head with approval, and then he said, "I take your jealousy. Forget it. It is mine."*

*The familiar darkbeast lightness soared around my body, and I laughed as my throat tingled with Caw's magic. My fingertips danced as I stroked my darkbeast's feathers in time to the music on the green.*

# Chapter Twelve

In the end I swept the floor at the bakery to get Goran his toffee bread. Back at the Travelers' camp I toted water from the city fountains—that was Goran's assigned duty for the day following his labor in Patrius's godhouse. When I worked for Keon, helping to prepare supper for all the Travelers, I saved the finest tidbits for Goran, but he declared himself too exhausted to sit by the cook fire. I brought his meal to Taggart's wagon, and I collected his wooden plate when he was through eating. He wasn't much recovered the next day, or the next, despite my waiting on him with all the care I would have given to the Primate.

That was when Vala decided he was faking.

I didn't believe her at first, but she said she would prove it.

The following morning Goran basked in the morning sun on the steps of Taggart's wagon. He had somehow summoned the strength to down four of the duck eggs Keon had boiled for breakfast. Vala came hurtling toward the wagon, her hair wild around her unwashed face. She choked on her words as she told Goran that Wart had somehow escaped, that the darkbeast toad had wriggled out of her cage and was hopping near the cook fires unattended. No one could corral her. Adding drama to the tale, Vala scarcely managed to gasp out "Bird!" before she clutched at an imagined stitch in her side.

Goran's strangled cry was like nothing I'd heard before. He raced to the cook fires, crying out for Wart, trying to save his darkbeast from some winged predator. Goran dropped to all fours, seeking out his slimy toad. He pushed cauldrons over, tugged at full barrels of flour, casks of oil, heavy rounds of cheese. He bellowed at a harmless swallow and threw a perfectly good apple at a huge crow that had the misfortune of paying too much attention to Keon's roasting spit.

At long last Vala produced Wart's battered cage from the shadows behind the smallest of the Travelers' wagons. Goran flew across the flagstones, screaming Wart's name, only to find that the toad squatted on her iron bed like a pulsing lump of cold meat. "Ach," Vala said, putting a lifetime of practice into the exasperated sound. "I must have been mistaken. Wart seems perfectly fine after all."

Goran shouted at Vala, using words I'd only heard the shepherds say back home in Silver Hollow. I rose to Vala's defense, shouting back with nicer speech, but I made it clear I was through waiting on a perfectly healthy boy. Vala laughed as Goran stormed off, and we both decided not to bring the prank to our own darkbeasts.

Goran didn't talk to us for two full days, until we were on the open road, well away from Rivermeet. Even then I had to bring him my slice of treacle tart to launch a conversation after we had helped make camp for the night. I forced Vala to come along because I was tired of the fight between the three of us.

"I won't stand for you again, Keara," Goran said. "Not with the Inquisitors." His voice was heavy; he actually sounded like he was making his own apology, even though his tone was resigned. "Polishing Patrius's altar was easy enough, but I'll not do that again. Not by choice." He shuddered. "And hopefully never by command."

"Why not?" Vala asked, licking traces of treacle from her palm before she picked up a stick to poke at the fire. A cascade of sparks danced toward the stars.

Goran shrugged and looked away from both of us before he said, "There were too many Lost people there. Men and women being taught the error of their worship."

I told myself I could not glance at Caw, even though I knew he was roosting on the wagon wheel behind me. I could give no hint that the Inquisitors had good reason to summon *me* before them for . . . teaching. "Error?" I asked, echoing the word as casually as I could.

Goran stared into the flames. "Blaspheming the gods," he whispered, as if merely naming the failing was as dangerous as action. "Ignoring Patrius's gloryday. Doing work instead of praying to the glory of the father of all the gods."

We all shuddered, captured by Goran's tone. Unexpectedly, Vala's darkbeast slid out of the darkness, creeping up her arm and coiling around her wrist. She had set Slither free when we made camp that night so that the beast could find her own supper; I had watched Vala tumble the darkbeast from her basket. Now my belly turned as I made out the lump of some undigested beastie beneath Slither's skin, some fresh prey working its way though the snake's body.

Nevertheless, Vala's fingers stroked her darkbeast's inky scales, as if she was calming herself by the automatic gesture. She might hate Slither, but the darkbeast was comfortable. Familiar. Safe.

Besides, Vala had to love the magic feeling that came from offering up a failing. Every child did. That was what kept us from rebelling, from refusing to take our worst thoughts and deeds to our darkbeasts. Even if Vala despised the snake that brought the sensation, she had to long for the feeling of lightness, the tingling certainty that she could float among the clouds.

I raised my own wrist, inviting Caw to take a perch. My breath came easier when he settled gently, taking care not to prick me with his talons. I curved my palm and stroked his back, smoothing the feathers as if he were a cat.

Vala whispered to Goran, "What did the Inquisitor make them do?"

I thought Goran might not answer her at all. When he finally did speak, his voice was so soft I had to lean into the cool darkness, away from the fire, just to hear what he had to say. "They wore chains," he said. "All of them."

"And?" Vala prompted. I gaped at her. I would not have had the courage to push for further details. I could hear the reluctance in Goran's voice, the true fear.

"And they were being punished."

When Goran seemed determined to say no more, Vala pinned him with her sternest look. Her steely, silent stare made me realize she was far more than just a pretty child. She was a hard, determined Traveler.

Goran spoke as if each syllable were being pulled from the depths of his belly. "The Inquisitor uses knives on all the Lost. And brands. He leaves his mark on bodies, as well as souls. And then he prays for them, repeating his words, over and over and over."

Caw fluttered to my shoulder, and I pulled my arms close around my knees, trying to stop the shiver that plucked my spine. When I blinked, I could see Bestius's priest behind my eyelids, his face contorted in fury after Caw escaped. I could picture my sisters and my cousins, my mother and my grandmother, all struggling to keep me safe, to keep me whole. To make me sacrifice Caw and take my rightful place in Silver Hollow, before the Inquisitors got involved.

"'And so we watched the night fall sweet and soft,'" Vala said, her voice rising and falling in the sing-song notes of a revel.

"'Mercy's blessings bearing cares aloft,'" Goran responded.

"What's that from?" My question sounded leaden in the darkness, as heavy as the bed of embers that anchored our fire.

"*Clementius and the Mariner,*" Vala said. "We performed the revel in Rivermeet. Weren't you listening?"

They'd performed a dozen revels in Rivermeet, Holy Plays and Common both. I couldn't learn all the words, not at the same time.

Vala shrugged and said, "I'll teach you the rhymes tomorrow. They're easy. You'll have them down by the time we get to Cooper Falls."

I lay awake long after Goran headed over to Taggart's wagon for the night. He said he had to check up on Wart, to make sure the toad was well fed. Beside me, Vala fell asleep quickly in the fresh air beneath the stars. I continued to worry at the problem of the Inquisitors and the Twelve, of my darkbeast and me. What was I going to do with Caw? How long could I stay with the Travelers? What would happen when I could no longer lie about my nameday, when I could not possibly pass for a child?

When I sighed for the thousandth time, Caw flapped down from the wagon, taking a seat beside my head. *"The Inquisitors aren't our real problem."*

*"What is?"* I formed my response as a silent thought, not wanting to disturb Vala any more than I already had with all my restless shifting.

*"The fact that I'm starving. You could have given me your treacle tart instead of saving it for Goran."*

I sighed. *"Hold your tongue, Caw, if you don't have anything useful to say."*

*"Ah! So now you order people around as if you were the Primate himself!"*

*"You're not people, Caw."* People were humans, men and women and children. People were tortured for becoming Lost.

My darkbeast ruffled his feathers, and I knew he was prompting me to apologize for my impertinent tone. I understood him as clearly as if he'd spoken the demand aloud. I had hurt his feelings, reminding him that he wasn't human, that he didn't deserve the rights and privileges of an actual person.

But I wasn't going to apologize. Caw should know how much I valued him—he was the very reason I lay there beneath the stars.

He was the reason I risked the Inquisitors' wrath. He was the reason I tossed and turned beside a fire, leagues from the only family I had ever known.

But that was not precisely true, I realized. I was leagues away from Silver Hollow, but not leagues away from family. Vala-ti slept beside me, having promised to teach me a revel. Goran-tu had stood for me before the Inquisitor. That was more than Robina or Morva would have done, if my actual blood sisters had been in Rivermeet.

Eventually Caw grew tired of my silence and took wing, but I sensed that he went only as far as the oak trees that ringed our campsite. If I'd wanted to, I could have reached for his thoughts. I could have apologized.

I didn't want to, though. Instead I lay awake beside the Travelers' fire, testing my memory of the revels' rhymed couplets until long after Mortana had climbed the horizon.

Caw wasn't back when I awoke in the morning. He stayed away while I broke my fast with a sweet millet cake. He made no appearance when I carried water from the nearby river, when I discovered a stash of fresh croneleaf, ready for harvesting. He gave no hint of his presence when Taggart stood on the top step of his wagon, raising his arms and commanding all the Travelers to gather around.

Goran crouched beside his grandfather, looking like a sly fox, ready to launch a game that could be won only with his own, secret rules. Vala huddled next to her father for once, both of them looking concerned, as if Taggart might share some terrible piece of bad news.

I stood alone.

"Eight weeks," Taggart said. He didn't raise his voice, but he pulled the words from the bottom of his chest, applying some Traveler's trick to make his tone the gravest I had ever heard. "Two months until the cath."

The troupe answered him with a hum of excitement. They wanted to know which revel they would offer up to the Primate, which would give them the best chance of traveling free for five full years.

I caught my breath, snagged by the quiver of expectation. Which play would Taggart choose in his bid to earn back the twelve silver coins he had spent to keep me from the Inquisitor? Would it be my favorite, *Nuntia and the Rainbow*?

Taggart proclaimed, "I had thought we would perform the revel of Patrius, the father of all the gods. That would remind Primate Hendor that he is lord over all his people, that we are all his to command."

There was a buzz of approval. It made sense to play to the Primate's pride, to honor him implicitly and explicitly at the cath.

Taggart shook his head. "But then I realized other troupes will likely do the same. Patrius is the easiest course, the most direct route across the broad plains of flattery. So I set aside that simple choice and considered instead that we should play the revel of Tempestia."

The goddess of weather, of sun and storms, of gales and lightning. *Tempestia and the Sheaf of Wheat* would have special meaning after the harvest, at the time of the Hunter's Moon.

"But I recalled that Lutecia was flooded in the first year of Hendor's reign. Tempestia long ago greeted the new Primate with a rough voice and a harsh judgment. No good comes from reminding a man of past disaster."

The Travelers shifted restlessly. They expected Taggart to be their leader, to make their difficult decisions for them. His admitting uncertainty made people as nervous as a cow forced to lead her herd back to the pen, without even a dog to guide her.

"And so I had another thought," Taggart drove on. "What has never been done in the cath, ever before? What has no troupe of Travelers ever dared to perform?" He waited several heartbeats, and I could feel the people asking themselves, *demanding* to know what new territory Taggart had espied. "We'll create a new Holy Play!" Taggart bellowed with all the force of a man who had lived his life upon a stage. "A revel of all the Twelve—all the gods on stage at once. *All* the gods, to honor Hendor. *All* the gods, to win the cath!"

Taggart's voice grew stronger each time he said the word "all." He raised his hands and clenched his fists, pulling down the very power of the oaks behind him. His ornate iron necklace trembled as he threw back his head; the decoration looked as if it had sprung to life with the very power of his declaration.

The Travelers exploded.

No one had ever created a new Holy Play, not since the days of First Primate Kerwen. Certainly, Common Plays were spun out every few years, new moral lessons about men and women, about the lives of ordinary people. But a new Holy Play? A unique text about the gods themselves? And all twelve of them, on one stage, in one revolutionary revel?

No one had dared to do such a thing for time out of mind. And no one had ever placed more than one god upon the stage at once.

Taggart elaborated: "Each of the Twelve will reveal a different aspect of our Primate. We'll show Hendor's strength as a gift from the gods, from all of them combined. We'll need to create new costumes, images of the Twelve that are united in color, in design. We'll make a whole new set of sigils—the familiar animals, of course, but crafted with a unity of line. We'll need new masks, each unique, but each part of a greater whole."

The Travelers were overcoming their shock, warming to the notion. I saw people nodding, a few determined smiles as performers began to envision a future that was different from all the pasts that had ever been.

Taggart rolled on. "And in this new revel we'll emphasize the glorious power of the Twelve. We'll contrast the gods with the story of a child, a questioner, a quester. We'll create an innocent, a wide-eyed villager who will gain a greater understanding of the Twelve, of Primate Hendor himself. And our new revel, our new guide, will carry us all to victory in the cath!"

I waited for everyone to look at me. I waited for them to realize that Taggart was talking about *my* life, *my* learning. Taggart was giving me a chance to redeem myself, to earn back the twelve silver coins he had paid to preserve me. My cheeks flushed as I anticipated the power of the Travelers' collective gaze. My lungs squeezed shut, and I had to remind myself to take a breath, to hold myself steady.

Taggart raised his hand. He was going to call me to the steps of his wagon. He was going to raise me up above all the other Travelers. I lifted my chin, welcoming the honor.

But the old man turned away. He extended his hand to his left. To Vala. "We'll build our tale around this one," he said. "Vala-ti will play our child."

I could not say which was stronger—the tide of embarrassment that washed over me or the tug of blind jealousy. I wanted to break for the trees, for the Great Road, for escape. And Caw chose that moment to swoop out of the forest. *"Ha!"* he thought, landing on my shoulder. *"You weren't expecting that, were you?"*

The surge of excited Travelers rolled me closer to Vala. I was standing in front of her. I had to say something, had to do something, had to *belong*. But I could not think of the right words, could not remember the most basic of polite gestures.

*"Vala-ti,"* Caw thought. *"I'm so happy for you."*

"Vala-ti," I managed to say, and my voice was only a little too tight. "I'm so happy for you."

*"I can't wait to watch you build the role,"* Caw thought.

"I can't wait to watch you build the role," I said.

*"Anything that I can tell you. Any way that I can help."*

"Anything that I can tell you." I was grateful Caw was there, that he was feeding me the words, giving me everything I needed to survive. I even managed to sound sincere as I said, "Any way that I can help."

Vala threw her arms around me, making Caw flutter to safety. "Thank you, Keara-ti!" she said, squeezing hard. But before she could say anything more, she was pulled away, surrounded by the Travelers, who were eager to offer their own congratulations.

I hugged my arms around me, feeling very much alone in the midst of all those people.

# Chapter Thirteen

I did my best to prepare Vala for her role. As the Travelers' wagons creaked from Rivermeet to Summerford, from Smithbridge to Bitter Falls, I told her tales about living in a village. I explained what it was like to share a single, stationary room with a mother and father, with two sisters. I described gathering at the communal oven to collect the weekly bread. I spoke about glorydays on the green, about honoring each of the Twelve with their unique rites, with their specific rituals.

Vala listened. She'd trained since birth to take on new roles, and she wasted no time learning to behave like a common villager. Her vowels were broader every time we spoke, and she took to ending her sentences with a gentle lilt that sounded as if she'd spent her entire life in the countryside. She set aside her brighter gowns, the bits of lace and flashy glass jewels that marked her as a Traveler. She learned to weave her curls into a single heavy braid that hung low against her nape.

There was more than that, though—more than words and clothes and hair. Vala carried herself differently when she acted like a villager. There was something about the set of her shoulders, about the way her hips moved as she walked.

Vala lost her Traveler's magic.

She became a girl like any other. She became boring and ordinary and . . . normal. And I was the one who taught her all of that. I was the one who fed her the Family Rule, who shaped her, who carved her into the new creature, more shocking because she was so very ordinary, so absolutely unremarkable.

Me.

The Travelers could not stage their newest revel without me. I found that *I* walked a little taller when I crossed the Travelers' camp. *I* held my shoulders back. *I* kept my chin up.

I had left behind the common life of a villager; I was no longer the everyday girl that Vala mimicked. In fact, I was now the very spine of Vala's success. I would be the reason the Travelers won the cath.

Which was all well and good, until Vala sat beside me at supper, examining me closely, as if I were some new herb to be tested and dissected and dried. "Wait," she said. "Turn toward me a little. Madrina bless us, is that *really* how you hold your spoon?"

"How else would I?" I stiffened as she stared at my hand. Madrina had nothing to do with it—that was just the way I ate my stew. There was nothing special about how I balanced the utensil against my bowl.

"It's just so curious. So different from how *we* do things."

We. The Travelers. Every time Vala examined me, I was forced to remember that I was different from my roadside companions. I was some sort of freak, like the Silver Hollow lamb born two springs before, the one with two heads that died before it could suckle even once.

Nevertheless, I knew I had something Vala did not. I had true knowledge. I had actual experience. And so I extended my arm, showing her the precise way I gripped my spoon. And I let her watch me chew, let her study how I swallowed. I was giving something back to the Travelers, to the folk who had spent twelve silvers to keep me out of the Inquisitor's grip, and I wasn't going to forget that. Even if my knowledge gnawed away at my heart. Even if I was jealous that Vala played the role while I played the silent, secret adviser.

"It's not fair," I said to Caw after one particularly galling afternoon. Vala had kept me walking around a clearing, lap after lap after lap, insisting that I moved my hips oddly, differently from everyone else she knew. By the time we finally returned to camp, in anticipation of Keon's supper bell, my back ached because I had hitched my gait, trying to work out what it was that Vala thought she saw.

*"What is not fair?"* Caw did not sound sympathetic as we watched the Travelers gather around the cook fires.

"Vala. She's treating me as if she were First Primate Kerwen's own daughter. If the Travelers wanted a village girl, they should have chosen one. They should have chosen me."

Caw bobbed his head up and down, obviously agreeing with me. *"You should do something about it."*

"Yes!" At last someone agreed with me. I repeated, "Yes, I should. But what?"

*"You could approach Keon right now and ask for an extra ration of apple tart."*

"What good will that do?" I almost shouted my protest. I lowered my voice to grumble, "How is apple tart going to help me play the lead?"

*"It won't,"* Caw said. *"But at least I won't be starving while I listen to you complain."*

I refused to talk to Caw for the rest of the evening, and I made a point of making him find his own supper in the woods. I gulped down every bite of my own apple tart, but it tasted bitter. Keon must have left some of the seeds in while it baked.

At least we didn't prepare for the cath all the time. Sometimes we spent an entire day doing something different. Outside of Amberdale we found a perfect cache of smooth stones to skip across the Silver River. Another day we collected firewood to trade for sweets in the next small village. Once, Vala bought me a length of red ribbon for my hair, and she spent an entire morning showing me how to work a complicated six-part braid.

And always, always, always we played tricks on Goran. Vala explained that the two of them had teased each other since they were infants. Neither saw any reason to stop, just because they traveled the Great Road.

Goran left worms in the toes of Vala's shoes. She put sand inside his water flask. He opened Slither's basket in the middle of the night. She hid Wart's cage inside one of the wagons.

I scarcely hesitated before joining in the fun. Ostensibly showing Vala how a village girl collected herbs, I added sheepleaf to Goran's tea. He couldn't taste it when he drank, but his sweat stank like manure for an entire week. Taggart made him sleep on the far side of the wagons, and no one would let him anywhere near the cooking fires.

Back and forth our games rolled. No one ever got hurt; we were truly only playing, filling the long days on the road. The other Travelers watched from a distance, never giving away our secrets (but never telling Vala and me what tricks Goran had played either). No one ever ordered us to take our wrongdoings to our darkbeasts. The Travelers had a different standard than Mother; they worried about different failings. Or else they didn't put much stock in darkbeasts at all.

Two weeks passed, and the Harvest Moon grew fat in the night sky. More than once I caught Vala staring at Slither's basket, her lips curling into an eager smile. One morning as we watched fog clear from the river's edge, Vala stooped down and thrust her hand into the chilly water. She held up her dripping treasure like an offering to the Twelve: a flat rock as big as her fist, worn smooth by the constant flow of water.

Somehow I knew she meant to use the stone to kill Slither.

At last the moon was one night shy of full. We camped in the tiny village of Three Rocks, where the Travelers' wagons filled the entire green. We performed a handful of skits after the sun set; there weren't enough villagers to bother with a complete revel. In fact, the place was so small it had only one godhouse— Pondera's wooden circle, on the southern edge of the clutch of cottages. There was no formal building devoted to Bestius.

Vala's nameday would start at dawn. I watched her place her rock beneath her pack, hiding it as if it were a precious thing. I thought of the night before my own nameday, the night before I was supposed to kill Caw. Even now my darkbeast perched on a wagon wheel behind me.

Then, I had wanted someone to talk to me. I had longed for anyone to tell me that I did not have to do what I had always been told was right, was just, was absolutely, completely necessary. I had ached for someone to say that I could love Caw, that I could save my darkbeast.

"Vala-ti," I whispered long after the camp had quieted around us. I spoke to her, but I looked at Caw.

"I'm awake," she said, her voice wrapped tight.

I imagined Caw as I had never seen him, lying dead and crushed and broken on Bestius's altar. "You don't have to do it," I said. "You don't have to kill her."

Caw made a noise deep in his throat. My heart began to pound. I was casting my entire future on those two short sentences. I was offering up all my hopes for staying with the Travelers, setting them in front of Vala, in front of my friend, in front of my adopted sister.

When I broke with convention, I had run away, had joined the Travelers. If Vala spared her darkbeast, where could the two of us go? Where could we take refuge from Bestius and the Inquisitors?

But Vala was not me. And Slither was not Caw. Vala's throaty laugh was warmer than the embers of the fire. "What is this? Some game you villagers play? One last dare before you claim your freedom?"

"Freedom?" I choked out.

Vala laughed again. "By Bestius's glory, you're a finer actor every day you stay with us! I could almost believe you want me to spare my filthy darkbeast. You want me to become Lost!"

*"Lost,"* Caw repeated, spiking the word deep into my skull.

Of course I should not have spoken to Vala. She did not understand. She could never understand. She was good and loyal and true, and she hated her darkbeast—like any normal child.

I forced myself to remember how the Travelers laughed, bringing the sound up from deep within their bellies. I used another of their tricks, curling up the corners of my mouth to force a true smile in front of my lying words. "You pass the test, Vala-ti. You're ready to take your place as a woman. You're ready to slay Slither forever."

She rolled over, and her deep, even breath soon told me she slept. But I stayed awake far into the night, after Venerius rose, after Mortana, after Recolta even. I stayed awake, and I thought about how close I had come to revealing my ugly, twisted truth.

Eventually, though, I must have slumbered, because the rollicking notes of a flute pulled me from dreams as dark as the inside of Bestius's godhouse. The sun was barely above the horizon. Automatically, I thought a greeting to Caw, but he was too far away to touch with my mind. No wonder, I remonstrated with myself. What darkbeast would want to hover near on a nameday gathering? What darkbeast would choose to bear witness to the destruction of his own kind?

Vala had no mother to dress her for her nameday, but the entire troupe served as family. Men and women gathered together—something they would never have done in Silver Hollow. They robed Vala in their finest costumes, cloth of gold for her dress and ermine for her cloak. A spangled crown rested on her hair, on the riotous black curls that Vala let tumble free for this one day, for this one morning when she was not practicing her role as village maiden. Face paints and golden bangles, embroidered slippers and jangling rings—Vala looked like an exotic creature by the time the troupe was done with her.

One thing was the same as my nameday, though. Vala was denied any breakfast, even the tiniest sip of water. Beneath her paints her face was pale as she made her way to the place of sacrifice. The village made do with a lambing shed converted into a space sacred to Bestius. The walls were stained black, in imitation of onyx slabs.

Taggart had sent ahead for a priest, summoning the man from some larger town down the road. The priest had blessed the dark shed, sketching Bestius's sigil of a fly in the dirt before the door. He'd thrown a handful of incense onto a brazier. The scent immediately transported me back to Silver Hollow, back to my own nameday ceremony.

The priest said some solemn words over Vala and Slither, reminding my friend that it was time for her to set aside the folly of childhood, to take up the mantle of being a woman. Vala offered up a nameday gift—a wooden brooch she had painted with the Travelers' false gold. The priest accepted the present gravely, as if it came from the Primate's own storehouse. He made a great show then of examining Vala's wrist, of making sure that she bore a tax tattoo, that the ink was bright enough to have been applied within the past year.

Everything was in order. Vala was ready. The priest's face was grave as he closed the shed door, locking in the child and her darkbeast.

I joined the other girls and boys, the children much younger than I, as soon as the door was shut. We ran around the building, chanting as loudly as we could: "Kill the darkbeast! Kill the darkbeast!"

Each time I said the words, my body felt heavier. My mouth was dry; it seemed as if fur clogged my throat. This was the opposite of darkbeast magic, a complete contrast to the airy release Caw gave me every time I brought him my failings.

Nevertheless, I performed a revel of sorts, acting out a role completely different from my own life, from anything and everything I believed. I sent a tendril of my thoughts toward Caw, trying to explain to him that I was playacting, just pretending, but he spoke no comforting words in reply. I wondered if he watched from some perch in the nearby trees.

I had no choice but to chase after Goran, to catch his rough hand in mine as we led another rousing chorus: "Kill the darkbeast! Kill the darkbeast!" With each circle around the lambing shed I felt a greater need to spit imagined sand out of my mouth.

And then, in an impossibly short time, Vala flung open the door of the improvised godhouse. She stood on the threshold, her arms stretched high above her. Slither was draped across her palms, a limp belt of shimmering scales marred only by a mash of red where a sleek head had been.

"Go forth, child of Bestius!" the priest proclaimed. "Go forth among your people! Do good and hate evil, and live as a righteous woman in the world!"

The Travelers' cheers echoed in the morning air, bolstered by the cries of the Three Rocks village folk. I surged forward, along with Goran, along with all the other children, eager to greet Vala, to congratulate her on her great deed well done.

But Vala did not spare me a glance as she strode away from the lambing shed. Her arms remained stiff above her head. Following some rule known only to the Travelers, she led the way back to camp. She wound between the wagons, crossing to a fire Keon had built to boil water for morning tea.

An expert on playing the crowd, Vala waited until everyone had gathered behind her. Only when the excitement was a physical thrum as thrilling as darkbeast magic, only then did

Vala cock her wrists. Taking careful aim, she threw the bloody remnants of her darkbeast into the very heart of the fire. There would be no keeping her former companion, as was the custom with village folk. Vala would have no tangible reminder of all the failings she had carried to her snake. She was a Traveler, after all, and she had no use for meaningless possessions, for useless objects carted from village to village, over all the roads of Duodecia.

Better to burn Slither. Better to forget.

"Vala Traveler!" Taggart exclaimed the title first, but everyone else took up the cry. The sound was overwhelming, echoing off the wagons, off the trees.

I still waited for Vala to look toward me, to catch my eyes above the crowd. But she did not. Instead she turned toward the women, toward the adult Travelers, who welcomed her with open arms, with petting hands and the murmur of a flock settling close. The women gathered around her, pulling her forward, guiding her up the steps of the nearest wagon. Even before the door shut, I heard a trill of laughter, a rollicking note that sounded as if they all were sharing a private joke. Women's words.

The men waited until the women were locked away, and then they moved about the camp, taking care of the work that must be done on that day, on any day, even a nameday. The children headed off to gather firewood, to play a hundred minor mischiefs.

Goran took a step toward me, started to say something, but then he looked away.

And I stared into the fire, watching the last of Slither's ashes crumble away to ebony dust.

*"Thank you,"* Caw whispered, and he tucked his wings in neatly as he settled on my shoulder.

I didn't ask him why he was thanking me. I didn't say anything. I merely transferred him to my wrist and stroked his gleaming feathers, ignoring the single tear that etched its way down my cheek.

# Chapter Fourteen

Three days later I was stroking Caw's feathers again, trying to gain courage as I passed through the fortified gate of Cooper Falls.

"Tall, isn't it?" Goran walked beside me as I tilted my head to look at the heavy blocks of stone above us. Each was stained black from the smoke of the torches that lit our way. Nervously I looked back at the iron teeth of the portcullis. I told myself that the people of Cooper Falls had no reason to trap me in the passageway beneath the walls. They did not know I was running from Inquisitors. They did not know I had spared my darkbeast.

"I'm not afraid," I said to Goran.

My voice shook, though, and he didn't bother to call me a liar.

Instead he merely waited for me to walk on. When I was finally able to convince my feet to move, he matched his gait to mine. At the same time he inhaled deeply, and then he exhaled on a count of five. I recognized the action as a Traveler's trick, a tool to prepare for a revel. When I imitated him, breath for breath, I immediately felt more at ease. Goran smiled—an open, sunny grin, absolutely without guile. We moved into the open air and the crowded streets beyond the guarded gate.

Cooper Falls sprawled before us—loud and stinking and seething with more people than I had ever imagined in one place. Stunned by the commotion, I squeezed my eyes shut. I tried to remember what Silver Hollow had looked like. I tried to picture the village green, and the play of sunlight through the branches that arched over Pondera's godhouse. I tried to recall the sweet-sharp-dusty scent of Mother's herbs, drying in the rafters of the cottage we had shared. I tried to remember the flavor of her seedcake.

*"You can always go home again."* Caw's tone was flat. My eyes popped open, and I was surprised to see my darkbeast's glare.

"No," I answered, and now I meant my stroking fingers to soothe him instead of me. "I can't. I'm not going anywhere without you."

*"You could take me back to Silver Hollow. Take my feathers, as a cloak. Take my claws, as clasps for a cape."*

"Don't even joke like that."

"*Who's joking?*"

I shuddered and told myself not to think about the past, not to dwell on the way that Mother had preserved her darkbeast, how she had kept the constant reminder of all the faults she had ever offered up. Vala's way had been better, destroying Slither completely.

Not that I was going to kill Caw. Ever.

Goran was staring at me oddly. He had heard only my half of the conversation. I forced a tight smile across my lips. "Come on," I said. "Let's follow the wagons."

Goran shrugged and stayed by my side as we wound our way through the city streets. The adults—including Vala, of course—hid inside the Travelers' carts, keeping their mysterious ways secret from the curious townsfolk. We children were free to move about, though, free to gape up at the buildings on either side of the wide street. Some of them reached three stories into the sky; the sun could not pry between their shadows.

I wondered if Vala missed seeing the wonder that was Cooper Falls. I missed sharing it with her.

At last we arrived at the market. A dozen streets flowed into one giant square, like rivers emptying into a lake. The wagon drivers lost no time threading their way across the broad expanse. Obviously familiar with the space, they blocked off one end of the market, carving out a corner for the Travelers' performances.

As soon as the horses were secured, the men began to haul out their trestles, setting the uprights that would anchor the wooden stage. Taggart waved his hands toward us children. "Go along, then. We want a full crowd by sunset."

By reflex, I looked for Vala. She would know where to find the wells in this town. She would guide us in the crying.

Except Vala wasn't a child any longer. She didn't cry the shows. She was responsible for setting out costumes, for lining up face paints. She had to practice her lines and prepare for the revel itself.

Goran pretended he hadn't seen me looking for my absent friend. He nodded toward Caw and spoke like we were in the middle of a conversation. "Are you taking him with you?"

Before I could answer, Caw took wing, seeking refuge on the peak of the tallest building that lined the market. "Be careful," I warned, worried that he was so visible in this strange place.

*"Precisely my suggestion for you,"* he said. *"But keep an eye out for treats. A sweet cake or two would be welcome, you know."*

I swallowed a smile and turned to Goran. "He'll stay here."

Goran squinted up at Caw. "That's one good thing about Wart. She doesn't go anywhere without my permission. I've never seen anyone give a darkbeast as much freedom as you do Caw."

I could not say whether the chill I felt was apprehension for Caw's safety, or the skirl of an autumn breeze through the shaded city streets. Before I could think of a solid reply, though, Goran took off at a lope, heading for a nearby lane. I broke into a run before I lost sight of him completely.

I thought I had learned how to cry a play with Vala. She had used Travelers' tricks, of course, making her voice boom loud, striding with power and grace as she moved through the streets. But ultimately she had made the Travelers' work seem ordinary, mundane, like such a part of daily life that people could not *avoid* coming to see us. Townsfolk bought bread. They pumped water. And they came to the market to watch the Travelers.

Goran had a completely different approach.

The first well we reached was ancient, a stone hovel shielding a decrepit pump. A half dozen women waited their turn for water, resting buckets on their hips, slumping with fatigue in the afternoon light.

Goran wasted no time scrambling to the top of the crumbling structure. He found toeholds where I saw none; he seemed to dig his thumbs into the stone as if it were heavy dough. When he reached the top of the well, he spread his feet wide, anchoring himself so that he could throw his arms up into the sky. "Good ladies of Cooper Falls!" he bellowed. His voice was so loud that I almost looked behind him, half expecting to find one of the full-grown Traveler men booming out the words. "Gather round, good ladies!"

At first the women fluttered away, cooing like doves in the sunset, startled and uncertain. One crone stepped forward, though, shielding her eyes against the sun. "And what are you selling, young rat?"

If Goran was offended by her words, he gave no sign. Instead he boasted, "I sell dreams, goodwife!"

"I've plenty of dreams," the old woman said. "I dream of a warm fire, and a full belly, and gold crowns in my pocket. Are you selling that, little rat?"

"My dreams are better than a bit of food, goodwife. Better than a few lengths of wood. Better even than gold."

"They must be grand indeed!" another woman shouted, and her words were met by laughter.

Goran lowered his voice then, pitching his words just quietly enough that every single woman had to take a step closer to hear. I even found myself moving forward, catching my breath in expectation.

"Aye, goodwife," he purred. "Imagine the Twelve, all gathered here in Cooper Falls. The Twelve, sharing all their wit and wisdom. All twelve gods, on a single stage, on a single night, in a single play."

A few of the women closed their eyes, as if they could see the revel Goran described. The oldest one, though, the wrinkled dame who had first spoken, called out, "Nonsense! You Travelers have no new workings. It's always the same plays. Perhaps a new gown here or a new robe there, but the words haven't changed since my grandmother's grandmother was a little girl."

"We've new words tonight, goodwife. I promise you." Goran turned his hands outward, palms up, as if he were a petitioner for mercy on the doorstep of Clementius's own house. He held his head forward just a bit. He opened his eyes wide. He looked the very picture of honesty, of earnest innocence, as he said, "We have words like birdsong, sweet with a hundred harmonies. We have words like a river flowing, through the rapids and over the falls. We have words like stars in the darkness, filling the nighttime sky."

And then Goran glanced at me, barely nodding. I recognized the command there. I had ridden with the Travelers for long enough that I understood a little of their power—the contrasts they worked. Goran had pulled the women's dreams into daylight; he had woven their hopes into castles of air, soaring as high as darkbeast magic.

It was my job to provide a foundation of earth.

"Believe him, good ladies. He speaks the truth." I kept my words blunt. Simple. Honest. "The people of Cooper Falls will be the first to hear our new play." I bowed my head, trying to appear humble. But I sneaked a glance through my lashes so that I could gauge the women's interest.

*That* one looked flattered, as if she believed that Cooper Falls was truly blessed, that the town rightly occupied a special place in the thoughts of all the Twelve. That other one looked suspicious; she did not believe me, did not think there was any reason for the gods to honor her home. And those three there—the young-est women at the well—looked thoughtful. They seemed to be weighing my words, calculating whom they could tell about the secrets the Travelers would share once the sun went down.

Goran looked satisfied as he jumped down from the well. "At sunset, goodwives," he said, and he strode away, not even looking back to be certain I was following him.

So it went as we traveled from well to well, from square to square, from godhouse to godhouse. Goran cast his line like an expert fisherman plunging into a well-stocked river. I set the hook, speaking to the townsfolk with familiar words, with simple affir-mations that I knew would draw them in.

By sunset the marketplace was filled with eager folk. Excite-ment rippled through the crowd—the Travelers' message had spread far and wide. I knew Goran and I had spoken to no more than threescore people during the day. But hundreds filled the cobbled square—men, women, and children. Every house in Cooper Falls must be empty, every shop and tavern bare of custom. The energy of the crowd crashed against the towering half-timbered buildings, rolled toward the stage, toward the Travelers.

For the first time since I had left the market to begin the cry-ing, I remembered Caw. I craned my neck and looked for him in the eaves of the building closest to the stage. I barely had time to recognize his sleek feathers against the dark timbers, though, before he swooped out of the gloaming. His claws bit deep into my shoulder as he landed, but I was so glad to see him I did not even think of crying out.

*"You've done your work well,"* he said. *"What a shame."*

"What do you mean?" I whispered.

But he did not answer. Instead he turned his attention toward the stage. The Travelers were starting the first public performance of their new revel. I looked toward *The Twelve.*

A curtain stretched across the stage, a shimmering length of silk shot through with crimson and gold, silver and blue, all the colors of the Twelve. Vala walked around the cloth, making it flutter in the breeze of her passing. Her hair was tamed into a single braid, and she wore a sturdy woolen apron over a long, drab skirt. She looked like half the women in the audience. She looked like I had, back in Silver Hollow.

I swallowed the familiar acid of jealousy, the bite of anger and frustration that *I* should be the person on that stage. *I* should have held the townsfolk captive, struck them breathless, snagged them in expectation of my very first words.

"Behold! I stand before you, common folk!" Vala's voice quavered, and she had to clear her throat.

I had never heard her sound so weak, so uncertain. "What's wrong with her?" I whispered to Goran.

He shrugged a reply that wasn't an answer. He took a step

forward, as if he meant to catch her attention, to steady her, as he had buoyed me in the dark tunnel entrance to Cooper Falls. Vala did not look down at either of us, though. Instead she stared out at the crowd from the front of the stage. She stood awkward and stiff, as if she had forgotten every lesson she had ever learned about performing.

I realized that I had not listened to Vala preparing for this role. She had spent all her time with the adults, all her time sequestered among the women. Goran and I had helped with other aspects of the new revel, stitching costumes, painting masks. But neither of us knew the first thing to expect about Vala's performance.

She raced through her lines. The tail end of every rhyme got lost in whispers from the crowd.

I wanted to stop the performance. I wanted to help Vala from the stage, to take her over to one of the cook fires. I wanted to throw a blanket over our heads, just the two of us, so that we could huddle shoulder to shoulder and talk and gossip and laugh until everything was the way it used to be, back on the road. Back before Three Rocks. Before Vala killed her darkbeast.

Of course I couldn't do any of that. All I could do was stare as Vala fumbled another rhyme. "What was that?" called an old man who stood near me at the back of the throng. "What did she say?"

Someone repeated the words, but the information got lost

in the flurry of excitement when the silk curtain was torn away, when it drifted down to the stage and off to one side. A pair of Travelers stood on the stage—Aurelius and Nuntia. The god of wealth and the goddess of messengers wore identical silken robes, swaths of cloth that hid the forms of their bodies. They were neither male nor female. They were divine, and they could be identified only by their sigils, by the ermine of Aurelius and the mare of Nuntia, each beast picked out in brilliant embroidery across the performing Traveler's chest.

Patrius came out next, and then Madrina. More gray robes. More embroidery, picking out the sigils. More voices, carefully held in a neutral register. The play went on, and every one of the Twelve appeared on stage. Their lines wove together—one god started a couplet, and his rhyme was provided by a goddess. The entire revel came together in a new way, telling a new story, weaving a new truth out of all the old tales.

For the first time in the history of Duodecia, all of the Twelve stood upon one stage. All of the Twelve told a single story.

Another Traveler trick emptied the stage at the end of the revel—each of the Twelve stepped back, slipping through a carefully hidden door in the bottom of the stage. As the gods disappeared, Vala was revealed at the back of the platform, looking very human and very ordinary and very, very much alone.

She had to clear her throat twice before she could manage the final couplet: "And if, good folk, you liked to hear our tale, go tell your friends to see us, without fail."

The crowd should have applauded. They should have shouted their approval. They should have stomped their feet and hollered for more.

Instead they merely stared at the stage. They peered at Vala, their faces twisted in absolute confusion. Some even seemed offended, as if they thought the Travelers mocked them for their simple faith. A few whispered to their fellows, and I heard some terrifying words—"godhouse" and "priest" and "Inquisitor." "Lost."

I was grateful I was not the Traveler there on display, stranded in front of everyone. I was not the person that everybody stared at, that everyone condemned. I was not the failure that Vala was, that the entire troupe had proven to be.

The crowd was nearly silent as they left the market. No one looked back at the Travelers. No one called for another play.

Caw dug into my shoulder for a firmer perch. *It seems that Cooper Falls does not appreciate the revel.*

Before I could respond, Taggart spoke from the stage, pitching his voice in a low and urgent whisper. He modulated perfectly, though. Every single one of the Travelers could hear. "In my wagon. Everyone. Now."

# Chapter Fifteen

I would never have thought that thirty-eight people—and one raven darkbeast—could fit inside a single Traveler's wagon. Taggart's ornate desk was folded up into the wall. Men leaned against the bolsters on his bed. Women sat on top of the decorated trunks. With Goran by my side, I actually crouched on the floor, beneath the bolted-down table. From that angle I could not see Taggart's face, but I could follow his bobbing iron necklace as he berated the entire company.

"What were you performing out there?"

Silence.

"It was only natural for our audience to fear something new!

Your mission was to convince them that our revel is too wondrous to fear!"

More silence.

"You must speak with confidence. You must believe your own rhymes. You must be certain that every single thing you say is true, that every last word rings with the unbridled power of all the Twelve!"

Absolute, rigid silence.

Taggart sighed, suddenly sounding a hundred years older than he was. "We're through here in Cooper Falls. We'll ride at dawn. Go now, and think about the Twelve, about everything you know this revel can be. Next time we'll make them understand."

The Travelers finally came to life. I heard one person suggest reworking the costumes. Another mentioned the masks, how they might be made brighter with dashes of silver paint. A third suggested tweaking an individual rhyme, and that thought led to a torrent about how several of the lines could be altered.

Taggart's grumbling sigh cut through the discussion. "Go, everyone. Sleep tonight. And tomorrow we'll rebuild our masterpiece for the cath." The wagon door opened, and we all gasped for a breath of fresh air. I nearly missed Taggart saying, "Vala, you stay behind. We need to talk."

Later that night, as I huddled beneath my blanket, missing my absent friend, I said to Caw, "What do you think Taggart said to Vala?"

*"He probably asked her if she prefers cream or jam on her scones."*

"I'm serious!"

*"So am I. I would never joke about scones."*

"Caw . . ."

He relented. *"Vala no longer has a darkbeast. Perhaps Taggart is guiding her as Slither once did. Helping her to find the spark of magic within her, magic that she can project upon the stage. Perhaps Taggart is helping Vala learn how she thinks, what she feels."*

"That's ridiculous. People don't talk about things like that."

Caw cocked his head. *"Really? I should think that people talk about things like that all the time."*

His surprise made me wonder. I had never spoken to Mother like that, putting words to my feelings. But maybe Goran did with Taggart—he seemed to like and trust the old man. And perhaps Vala was used to speaking with Keon. And to Taggart—she had stayed behind without protest.

I pulled my blanket up to my chin, then wrapped my arms closer around my body. Mother and I should have spoken more, back in Silver Hollow. We might have, if Father had not died in the vineyard. If Robina had not been the firstborn, the strong-willed, perfect daughter. If Morva had not been so sweet and good.

I thought about the day I left Silver Hollow. Mother had spoken to me then. She had tried to convince me to track down Caw.

She had discussed good behavior and bad. What other conversations might we have had if I had stayed?

I would never know, of course. Because staying would have meant losing Caw.

I never found out what Taggart said to Vala. I was asleep before she finally left the wagon, and she might not have spoken to me even if I had stayed awake. Not now. Not since she had killed her darkbeast and become an adult. The next morning, though, Goran said that Vala was weeping when she crossed the courtyard.

I wondered if she missed Slither, even a little. If she longed for a darkbeast so that she could offer up her sorrow. At least then she would be able to feel the darkbeast magic. The lightness of freedom. The joy of being good.

As Taggart had commanded, we left Cooper Falls as soon as the city gates opened. We spent three nights camped beside the Silver River, eating dry bread and cheese, spending every instant of daylight reworking the costumes, adding embroidery, decorating the sigils with brilliant feathers and fur and other exotic details.

I pitched in where I could. Goran did as well. In fact, he and I spent an entire afternoon gluing glass jewels to the gods' matching masks. The work was boring, but we could look back at our progress, could easily see the contribution we had made. Caw enjoyed the way the light caught on the colored stones; he was so distracted by the jewels that he forgot to beg for treats. I might not have thought about feeding him at all if Goran had not taken a break just before sunset.

"Where are you going?" I asked. We still had three masks to finish.

Goran looked embarrassed. He waved a deceptively casual hand toward the riverbank. "I need to dig for worms. For Wart. They burrow too deep after the sun goes down."

I was so astonished I could not think of an answer, not until Goran had left for the water's edge. "Caw?" I finally asked. "What do you make of that?"

My darkbeast did not bother staring after Goran. *"What do I make of a child caring for his darkbeast? Nothing. Nothing at all. At least* one *animal in this camp is going to get a treat tonight."*

I didn't even bother to retort. Caw had eaten more treats in his long life than all the other darkbeasts combined—at least all the darkbeasts *I* had ever met.

Goran came back to help with the masks after he had fed Wart. His face was shuttered, though, and I dared not tease him about his newfound sense of responsibility. Nevertheless, Caw made a thrumming sound deep in his throat, as if he approved of Wart's being spoiled.

We arrived in the village of Heartsmead, a midsize settlement where the Travelers rarely stopped. Goran and I traveled from cottage to cottage, telling the fine people that they were special, that they were chosen, that we had created our newest revel just for them. And, somewhere between the green and the outermost home, I realized our words were true—*we* had created the revel. I was one of the Travelers now, bound to them in success and in failure.

Alas, the Heartsmead villagers were also confused by the sight of all the Twelve on stage at once. During the performance a handful of children asked questions in sad, uncertain voices, tugging at the hems of their parents' garments.

I realized that the people of Heartsmead were lost because we had dared to create a new Holy Play. Everyone knew—or *thought* they knew—that there could be no new Holy Plays. There had not been for centuries. If Travelers performed a piece about the gods, they performed one of the twelve familiar revels.

Until now.

That was the genius behind Taggart's idea. We were presenting the Twelve in a new light. We were inviting our audience to experience their religion with fresh eyes, to discover new things about the gods and goddesses who controlled our lives. We were making something new, something daring. Something novel enough to win the cath.

That night Taggart ordered us to his wagon, again. He demanded that the entire troupe rework the play, again. He insisted that the costumes be recut, again, that the stitches be rewoven, again.

Rushing Falls hated the revel. Long Lake, too. In Smith Crossing they started shouting partway through the show. We never got the chance to finish the play, to make the Twelve disappear, to force poor Vala to deliver her final lines, abandoned in the center of the stage.

After that last disaster Taggart did not say a word. He merely stalked across the green. He slammed his wagon door. He stayed inside for the rest of the night, tallow candles burning bright in the window. Each of the Travelers stared at the star-washed sky, obviously wondering what we could say, what we could do, how we could refashion the revel to win the cath.

Sometime after midnight Goran drifted up to my side. He nodded at Caw, as if he were extending a formal greeting to the darkbeast sitting on the wagon wheel behind me. Settling on his haunches, Goran poked at the fire, releasing a cloud of sparks that swarmed in front of us like angry gnats. "I didn't think Vala could be any worse," he said.

I glanced at the women's wagon. Not for the first time, I wondered what they talked about in there, especially on these long nights, when we seemed surrounded by folly and loss and disaster. They must be pulling out all of the old embroidery on the costumes, ripping away the careful stitches that had taken so many long hours to complete just the night before. Their fingers must be sore from so much time with the needle. Their eyes must be tired.

"It's not Vala's fault," I said. The words were pulled out of some place deep in my chest. I didn't want to say them. I didn't even want to think them. Vala wasn't the best Traveler for the role; if she were, she could have opened the play in a way that gripped the audience. She could have delivered her last lines with enough drama, enough power, that everyone would understand.

I would be better at speaking those lines.

Except I wouldn't be. The revel itself was flawed. The entire play was damaged. Dangerous. It took truths that every person knew and turned them upside down, inside out. It destroyed all the peace and order and harmony that any of us had ever known about the Twelve.

Goran poked at the fire again. "It all started the night she killed Slither." He swallowed hard and looked away. "It's like she's forgotten the feeling, the lightness, from when her darkbeast took a wrong. She's *heavy* on the stage, like a stone sinking through water."

I nodded. I would not have thought to phrase it that way, but Goran was right. Vala had lost the joy of performing. She had lost the hum and the tingle, the breath of life she had always shown before.

Goran shoved his stick deeper into the fire, releasing another spiral of sparks. "Maybe we shouldn't kill our darkbeasts," he said. "Not if we're ruined as performers."

Caw twisted his neck, stretching to preen some difficult feathers on his back. *"Listen to this one,"* he thought. *"He is wise."*

I rolled my eyes before returning my attention to Goran. "This isn't only about Slither. Vala can't help what the audience thinks. It's the way we're presenting the Twelve that disturbs them."

Goran nodded. "They're afraid to see something new. Something different. They don't like being asked to think in ways they've never thought before."

*"Very, very wise,"* Caw thought.

"What are we going to do?" I asked Goran.

"Rework the revel tomorrow. Write new lines. Again."

I sighed and pulled my blanket up over my shoulders. It was nearly dawn before I fell asleep.

As Mortana crested the horizon, I whispered to my sleeping darkbeast, "Caw."

*"Treats?"* he thought sleepily.

I ignored his constant quest for food. "How did you know?" I asked. "Before the revel in Cooper Falls. You said 'what a shame' when you saw the size of the crowd."

*"I'd watched the new revel. Watched them all rehearse."*

"And?"

*"And Taggart said it that night. Like Goran did yesterday. Humans fear new things."*

"Not me."

"*Not you,*" he agreed. But then he said, "*Vala, though. She's afraid.*"

"Afraid of what?" The Vala who had been my friend had never been afraid.

"*A world without Slither. A world where she—and she alone—is responsible for her actions.*"

That didn't make any sense. Vala had always been responsible for her actions—including the decision to kill Slither. Just as I was responsible for saving Caw.

But then I started to see the truth behind Caw's words. All her life, ever since she was twelve days old, Vala had been told that Slither would take away her negative emotions—fear and pride and rage. All her life she had believed in the absolute power of her darkbeast to cleanse her, to give her that precious feeling of freedom. Slither had made her feel good. Slither had made her *be* good.

And now Vala was stranded without her darkbeast, without her familiar friend.

No. Not friend. Slither had never been Vala's *friend*. But the snake had been a comfort. A support. A solid base in a life where everything else changed every day that Vala grew from a baby into a child into a young woman. Every day that she traveled the Great Road.

With Slither gone Vala was forced to face her bad feelings by herself. She could no longer offer them up, let Slither take them. She had to manage on her own—anger and jealousy, fear and sorrow.

Certainly, Vala was a believer. She thought she was better than I, that she had mastered more lessons because she had killed Slither. In truth, though, we were exactly the same. We were both twelve-year-old girls, hoping to make the Travelers' latest revel a success.

But only Vala was suffering the loss of her darkbeast—a loss that left her alone, off-kilter. Utterly confused on stage. I couldn't explain it completely, but the truth was there for everyone to see every time she spoke her lines.

As it turned out, she had ample opportunity to practice those lines over the next five days. We reworked the entire revel yet again. Every single word was changed. I could no longer tell whether the play was better or worse than it had been. I could no longer judge the Travelers' work.

Greenvale was the largest town we had seen since Cooper Falls. It reminded me of Rivermeet, with its tight clutch of buildings, its numerous godhouses, each sheltered within a well-groomed courtyard.

We passed Bestius's low, black structure toward the heart of the town. As the wagons crept by, I thought of the rhymed couplets that announced the god's arrival on stage, the eleventh of all the deities to look out at the audience. I knew every word he said, both in the current version of the revel and every one that had gone before. A shudder combed my spine, equal parts fatigue from the revel and fear of the god discovering I had spared my darkbeast.

As if summoned by my worry, there were a dozen Inquisitors waiting for us in the marketplace.

# Chapter Sixteen

By camping beside the river for five full days, we had given people time to talk. Birds must have flown as well, messengers carrying warnings to godhouses, to priests and priestesses. My belly turned to water as I saw the assembled cloud white robes. Each face was hidden, but I could imagine the hawk-eyed glares directed at me, at all of the Travelers. The Inquisitors' hands were tucked inside their sleeves, but I pictured chains held taught, knives bared and waiting.

The Inquisitors were not alone. Dozens of men and women stood behind the white-robed religious figures, huddled in their common wool, their worn leather. Goran and I would not need to cry Greenvale. Everyone had already gathered for the revel.

The revel, or whatever other entertainment the Travelers would provide.

Taggart took his time emerging from his wagon. When he did finally open the door, he stepped forward with calculated nonchalance. Any of the townsfolk would think he just happened to pause at *that* spot on the steps. They would think coincidence made him choose *that* particular crimson robe. They would conclude that mere chance made his beard billow over his ironwork necklace in *that* precise pattern.

But I knew differently. I had been with the Travelers long enough to recognize the reason behind everything Taggart did. His stopping in that precise position framed him in front of the massive wagon, lent size and strength to his own broad shoulders. His crimson robe hinted at the power of the Primate, our lord and leader who would be honored with our finest words at the cath, only two weeks away. The gray of his beard contrasted with the iron of the necklace, the intricate swirls making him seem older and wiser and more worthy of respect.

As if to emphasize Taggart's power over the darkbeast world, Caw chose that moment to fly from my shoulder. He landed on the wagon wheel closest to Taggart's shoulder, and I was certain I saw his head dip in fealty to the Traveler. *"Come back here!"* I thought to Caw as sharply as I could.

My darkbeast did not stir, though. Instead he gazed at Taggart with the level of intensity he usually saved for food. The power of Caw's stare was so great that I *had* to look at the old man. Even as I shifted my attention, I wondered how many other eyes had been directed to Taggart as well.

"My lords," Taggart said at last, pitching his voice perfectly, making each clear syllable heard by all the watching townsfolk. "How may we humble Travelers serve you?"

The tallest of the Inquisitors stepped forward. "We have heard about your play. We wish to see your work, and to judge whether you speak heresy before the Twelve. We must determine whether all of you are Lost." He sounded old—ancient, even—but his spine was straight, his shoulders thrown back.

Taggart nodded, as if he had expected those exact words. "We will present our work this very night. After sunset, as is the tradition for all Travelers."

"We will see it now." The Inquisitor offered no room for argument, no space for protest.

"My people are weary," Taggart said. "We have traveled long upon the Great Road."

"Your people have spent five days camped beside the Silver. You will show your play now, or not at all."

Taggart's jaw tightened as he looked out at the twelve robed men, at the restless crowd behind them. His eyes narrowed, as if he counted the people ranged against him, as if he weighed the strength of their opposition, the heat of their anger. "Very well," he said at last. "If we may have until noon to prepare our stage, our costumes." The Inquisitor started to speak, but Taggart cut him off. "That is, if you wish to see our newest revel. We can perform another work without delay, without any preparation at all."

"Noon," the Inquisitor said, and venom dripped from the single word. His hands flashed from his sleeves for just an instant, and he brought his palms together in a single resounding clap. Each of his robed companions marched to a point on the edge of the market, distributing themselves as evenly as the petals on a sunray flower.

Taggart did not need to clap to send the Travelers to their stations. In grim silence the men began to build the stage. The women set out costumes and paint. I looked to Goran even as he met my eyes. We had no job, with the entire town already gathered in the marketplace. He jerked his chin toward the closest of the wagons. We huddled by the wheels, trying to stay out of everyone's way.

"What do you think they mean to . . . ," I started to ask, but he shook his head. The closest Inquisitor was turned toward us. His face remained hidden, but I was suddenly certain he was listening to my every word.

"We'll sit here," Goran said, as if I had asked him how I could best assist our fellow Travelers. "We'll sit and wait for Taggart to give us a command."

"Sit and wait." The voice came from above us—familiar, although I had never heard it dripping with so much anger.

"Vala!" I said.

"Of course you two will *sit and wait*." Her lips were chapped, and the skin beside her eyes stretched tight. Her face was very pale, except for a bright red flush that bloomed high on her cheeks.

"What else would you have us do?" Goran asked. He pitched his voice to be soothing and kind, as if he wanted to help Vala. If he'd been closer to me, I might have stomped on his foot. I did not want him helping Vala. I did not want him assisting her with anything. She had spent nearly a fortnight ignoring us. Goran was *my* friend now. Vala had no right to him, to his attention.

"I suppose I should be grateful," she said, and I don't think she even realized she had not answered Goran's question. "I should be pleased that neither of you is crying the show. You always bring in the wrong sort of audience, the weak-minded people, the fools who can't possibly understand what we're doing with the new revel."

"Vala," Goran said, and his voice was a little tighter. "We cried the shows as best we could."

"That wasn't good enough, though, was it?"

My answer burned out of me before I could think about the weight of the individual words. "We brought you the people who were there! It's not our fault you couldn't say your lines!"

Vala's shriek was empty of words, the bare cry of a mindless animal. She launched herself at me, her fingers curved like Caw's talons. I stood my ground, all the days of jealousy and anger rooting my feet. My own hands stiffened as I tried to scratch back at her too-pale face. Goran tried to thrust his body between us, but Vala reached around him, clawing at me like a madwoman. All of us were grunting like hungry pigs.

"Enough!"

My ears rang with the shouted word. I opened my mouth, working my jaw, trying to get my hearing back in order. Dazed, confused, I blinked hard, and I saw Taggart towering over the three of us. "Enough, all of you! Do you not realize we have a real threat among us? Do you not see that your troupe needs you now?"

My cheeks burned with embarrassment, and I was certain every single person in the market was staring at me. I tried to think of something to say, of some excuse to offer, but I seemed to have forgotten my words.

"Keara! Into the wagon with you. Take this to your darkbeast!"

I wanted to tell Taggart I had not started the fight. Vala had, Vala who was a woman, Vala who had already done away with her darkbeast, but who clearly had lessons left to master.

The old Traveler's eyes were flashing, though, and the cords in his neck stood out like ancient vines. Furious, I collected Caw from the wheel and ducked inside the dark wagon. I slammed the door and threw myself onto one of the bolted chairs. "It wasn't my fault," I said.

*"Vala is frightened."*

"I can't do anything about that. I can't make her remember her lines."

*"She is your friend."*

"Was. She isn't my friend anymore. She tried to kill me out there."

*"Let's not be dramatic."*

"I'm not being dramatic!" But even as I shouted the words, I realized I was overreacting. I was shaking, trembling in the aftermath of the fight that Vala and I had not finished. "All right. Maybe I am. Just a little." Caw waited. "All right. A lot. But . . ."

*"But?"* he asked when I stumbled to a stop.

I thought for a long time. There wasn't anything else for me to say. Vala was terrified that the only life she had ever known was ruined, that everything she had ever wished for, everything she had ever desired, would be taken away—by the Inquisitors, by the townsfolk, even by her own troupe, if Taggart took away her role. She truly was lost—not in the terrifying sense that the Inquisitors meant. But in the ordinary sense, of a person who had lost her way. A person who needed to be guided home.

"You're right," I finally said. "I was wrong." I waited for my darkbeast's familiar words: "I take your . . ." What? Anger?

Jealousy? Selfishness? All of those, and more, and less. "Caw?" I whispered.

*"I'm thinking."*

"Thinking of what?"

*"Thinking of how much Taggart wanted you out of that market square, enough to send you here, to his private space. I'm thinking of how many Inquisitors are waiting out there. I'm thinking of how many messenger birds might have flown this far north, how many people might be looking for a village girl who failed to kill her darkbeast on her nameday more than two months ago."*

With every word Caw placed inside my skull, my skin grew colder. My lungs froze. I could not breathe, and my teeth began to chatter. "That's im-impossible," I finally said. "Taggart doesn't know. He *c-cannot* know." Caw, though, did not say anything. He understood that neither of us could say what Taggart had or had not learned about our past. "Caw," I whispered. "What are we going to do?"

*"For now we'll sit here. The leader of your troupe instructed you to take your failings to your darkbeast. You have no choice but to wait until your darkbeast takes those flaws. You must sit, and wait, in silence."*

I heard two words he did not speak: *In safety.* I folded my arms across my chest and tried to convince myself not to worry, even as I heard the Travelers start their revel in the marketplace.

PART FOUR

# Despair

*I was eleven years old. The spring rains had come on time, but they had not stopped. We were two weeks past the Planting Moon, and still the rain fell every day. The shepherds picked sprouted plants out of the wool on each sheep's back. A carpet of moss slicked the stone steps that led to our cottage. My chest was tight with a heavy cough, and my scalp prickled with sweat from a fever.*

*Mother sent me to the ovens to collect our weekly bread. I tried to shelter the loaves beneath my apron, but the corner of one was mush by the time I crossed our threshold. Mother sighed and tore off the damaged bit, stirring it into a mug of milk along with a dollop of honey and a healthy dose of willow bark tea. "Drink," she said, refusing to listen to my protests. I started to cough as I swallowed, and more of the milk ended up on the hearth than in my belly.*

"Sleep," Mother told me, sending me back to the bed that we shared. "Sleep will heal your cough better than any herbs I can give you."

I lay down on the mattress, but the sheets felt clammy against my skin. I wondered if my hair was ever going to be dry again.

A leak woke me out of a tangled nightmare, a terrifying dream where the drumbeat of the rain merged with the crash of boulders tumbling down the riverbed. They rolled through Silver Hollow until they came to rest at our cottage door, blocking me in forever.

Drip. Drip. Drip.

My eyes were gritty. When I swallowed, it felt like knives carved the inside of my throat. My head spun as I sat up. I staggered to my feet and managed half a dozen paces, the cottage tilting oddly around me.

Drip. Drip. Drip.

The rain had finally twined its watery fingers through our thatched roof. Water glistened along the cottage's central beam, gleaming like oil in the flickering firelight. Mother's braids of applemint and sweetbreath were ruined. Her entire stock of lacemallow had turned to sludge, all of the feathery fronds I had dried so carefully by the fire the autumn before, turning them every evening, night after night after night.

Drip. Drip. Drip.

I started to sob. At first there was just a hiccup, a tiny noise that drowned in the rain's constant drumbeat. I took a deep breath, thinking to steady myself, but a full-blown cough snagged my chest. The last of my *resolve shattered like an earthen dam giving way beneath a raging river. One last time I tried to catch my breath with a great, shuddering gasp. When I realized I couldn't stop myself, I panicked and wept even harder.*

*I didn't hear Mother enter the cottage. I didn't feel the draft of the door opening and closing. I didn't smell the wet-sheep stink of her soaked cloak.*

*"Keara-ti," she said, but I did not answer. I could not; I was too lost in my own desperate world. I was certain that the rain would never end, that all of Mother's herbs were ruined, that our lives were destroyed forever. "Keara-ti!" she repeated.*

*"No," I choked out. "It's all lost. There's nothing left."*

*She guided me back to the bed and tried to make me sit beside her. I fought, though, pushing back with my little remaining strength. "Hush," she said. "It will be fine, Keara-ti. Don't worry."*

*"You don't understand! The rain ruined everything!"*

*She settled her palms against my cheeks, as if her calloused flesh could absorb my panic. "No, Keara-ti. I tell you, this will pass."*

*I thrashed my way free. "No! This is the end! We'll all die, like Father died!"*

*"Enough, Keara-ti!" Mother's gentle touch gave way to iron words. "You rave like a child who has never heard of the Twelve. You have no faith! Take your despair to your darkbeast."*

*She could not make me stand by Caw's cage. I was too tired. I shivered too hard, despite the fire burning high on the hearth.*

*Instead Mother carried Caw's cage to the bed. She slipped the worn leash around my wrist and eased me back onto the pallet. Then she tucked the blanket around my shoulders before heading back into the storm.*

"I was sleeping," *Caw said grumpily.* "That's the easiest way to wait out a storm, you know."

*"You'll sleep forever, then. This storm is never going to end."*

"Aye. The rain will never cease. We'll all build boats and sail from village to village. The Primate himself will leave golden Lutecia and rule from the very center of the high seas."

*"That could happen." My words were thick; I could barely push them past my clogged nose, out of the congestion that weighted my chest.*

"And if it did, then your mother would find new plants, in the sea. She would learn other ways to heal."

*"There are no other ways."*

"You know so much, do you? You have become so wise, in all your years of living?"

*"I know enough to understand we're all doomed."*

"Were you doomed when the fire scorched the oak grove last summer?"

*"That was different. Everyone knows that firecap blooms after a fire. People came to Silver Hollow just to buy Mother's stock after the oak trees burned."*

"And were you doomed when the river flooded its banks three springs past?"

Chagrined, I admitted, "The floods brought fresh soil to the river-banks. Mother had the best harvest of goldenfloss since she's been collecting."

"And the rockslide, last winter, high up on the slopes?"

"Snowlap," I said. The rocks had ripped up the hearty roots, sweeping the rare herb into the upper sheep pastures, where Mother could collect it for the first time in a generation.

"Then why would this rain be different? Why is this rain the end of the world? Why would you despair now?"

I shook my head. Now, with Caw laying out the facts before me, I realized I had acted foolishly. "I should build up the fire," I said. "Lay out the lacemallow. Dry it again so that Mother can use it."

Caw bobbed his head approvingly, but he said, "There will be time enough to build the fire later. For now, get your sleep. You'll feel better by the morning."

"How can you know that?" I thought the words instead of saying them, my lungs too weary to force out further speech.

"Your breathing has settled, deep in your chest. The grippe is yielding. I can hear the difference. You'll feel it by dawn."

I drew the deepest breath I could, trying to measure the relief Caw promised. As I exhaled, I heard him whisper deep in my mind, "I take your despair. Forget it. It is mine."

I was too tired to float free with Caw's words. Nevertheless, his formula vibrated through me, humming deep inside my bones.

Caw was right. My fever had broken by morning.

# Chapter Seventeen

Caw made no pretense about evaluating my flaws, about considering whether to take them and make them his. Instead he flew to the top of the iron lantern and hunched his head into his neck. He appeared to fall asleep immediately.

It was difficult for me to stay in hiding. Outside the wagon the Travelers started to present the most recent incarnation of the revel. If I closed my eyes, I could picture Vala standing at the center of the stage, lost and alone as she delivered her lines. I could imagine each of the Twelve joining her. I could envision the crowd gathered in the marketplace, the townspeople standing in their common clothes, uneasy at the new words, uncertain about the new performance.

And I could see the Inquisitors surrounding everyone, like towering walls looming over a frightened, cowering city.

The revel ended. I could make out the rhythm of Vala's voice speaking her last lines, but I could not distinguish the individual words. Alas, there was no applause. There was no sign that the folk of Greenvale—that the *Inquisitors*—had embraced a single word of the Travelers' new Holy Play.

I smelled the smoke before I heard the fire. Oak was burning.

I heard scrambling about the Travelers' camp then. Heavy trunks opened and closed. Women's voices rose in complaint. Men shouted out protests. Children's feet pounded past my wagon, first in one direction, then in another.

"Caw," I finally whispered. "I have to see what's happening."

His response was surprisingly alert, and I realized he had faked his sleeping. *"You won't change anything."*

"That doesn't matter. The Travelers are my people now. I have to know."

*"Do what you must."* Caw hunched down on the lantern again, and I crept to the door. I counted to one hundred as I eased the latch open—slowly, slowly, ever more slowly. I was determined that no one would see the change, no one could possibly notice me emerging from the wagon.

I had barely gotten my head out the door when I realized what was happening.

A bonfire filled the center of the market. The flames were bedded in a vast field of glowing embers; orange and yellow tongues licked higher than the tallest man. In fact, the fire was surrounded by a dozen tall men—the Inquisitors were arrayed around the conflagration. The fire's heat whipped their snow-white robes.

Broad planks burned in the heart of the flames. Glancing around the market, I finally recognized the fuel. The Travelers' stage was already nearly completely destroyed.

As I watched, the lead Inquisitor barked out a harsh command. A woman stepped forward, the Traveler who had played Nuntia. She raised a bundle high above her head and balanced it for a long moment. I realized that she held her costume, the precious gray silks that had been sewn and resewn, decorated over and over again with delicate embroidery. Another shout from the Inquisitor, and the Traveler tensed her wrists and sent the costume hurtling into the heart of the flame.

Another command, and another Traveler stepped forward. This one held Aurelius's robes. The god of wealth was consigned to the fire with scarcely a hesitation.

Recolta. Venerius. Mortana. Patrius. Madrina. Clementius. Tempestia. Pondera. Marius. Bestius. Each of the Twelve was summoned from the knot of Travelers. Each performer was forced to surrender a costume. Each was commanded to destroy the silk and thread, the beauty that had been unique to our revel, unique to our new Holy Play.

The sigils came next, after all the costumes were destroyed. Feathers and fur, gold paint and glinting glass, each animal sacred to the Twelve was sacrificed. The face paints, too, and the long silken curtains, all of them, consigned to the flames. Delicate ash floated high above the chanting crowd of townsfolk, turning angry faces black with soot.

At last there was only one Traveler left, one young woman who had not offered up her vanity, who had not burned her flawed remnants of the revel. She stood before the fire, silhouetted in nothing more than a rough linen shift. Her black curls flew wild around her face, as if they caught the very soul of the bitter smoke that wafted far above the marketplace.

Looking neither left nor right, the young woman hefted a bundle into the fire. She flung it with all her strength. The cloth came loose as she threw it, streaming in the fire wind like a ragged woolen banner—a common apron, a rough-spun skirt.

Vala stared at her costume long after it caught fire and flared, long after its final ashes drifted away on the wind.

The lead Inquisitor's voice boomed over the crackle of the fire. A crazed part of my brain registered that he spoke as loudly as any Traveler, that he could have taken the stage in any corner of Duodecia, commanded any audience. "The fire has taken your blasphemy, Travelers. The Twelve will never again stand together upon a single stage. The Twelve will never again be devalued by weak and common men, worked into a new and unproven Holy Play." He glared at Taggart. "Keep watch over the fire. Rake the ashes. And never show your face in Greenvale from this day forth, lest all of you be declared Lost for now and forever." He raised his hands, as if he would call down the wrath of all the gods himself. "And let all proclaim the mercy of the Twelve."

I understood the formula. I knew what I was supposed to say, I and every other person who heard the Inquisitor's pious proclamation. But I barely had the heart to add my whisper to the vehement chant of the Greenvale townsfolk. "Let all proclaim the mercy of the Twelve!"

Behind me, in the wagon, Caw remained conspicuously silent.

We were a sorry procession, heading out of Greenvale. We had all our horses, and the wagons, of course. But the empty carts were light on the road, clanking and clattering like forlorn ghosts as we remembered the finely crafted goods we had lost—our stage, our costumes, the sigils of the Twelve.

"What are we going to do, Caw?"

*"We certainly can't bake sweetcakes if we keep rolling along this road. Perhaps we can trade for scones at the next village. You could offer up the words of a revel or two, even without the trappings of a full play.*

*That should be good for* something. *Probably not raisins, though. Or apples. Those are too sweet for someone to give away for words alone.*"

"You know I'm not talking about treats!" Why did I even bother talking to Caw? Why did I ever trust him with anything serious? Anything important? How could he laugh about sweets when the Travelers' world was coming to an end?

*"Sometimes we have to laugh,"* Caw said, as if he had heard my silent ranting. Of course, being my darkbeast, he had. *"Sometimes we have to laugh so that we do not cry."*

I had no answer for that.

No one bartered for scones in the next village.

The teeth-jarring rattle made it difficult to think, difficult to plan what we could possibly do next. I had kindled the Travelers' financial woes weeks before, when Taggart paid the Rivermeet Inquisitor twelve silver coins, the bribe that I had unwittingly triggered. And now, with our entire revel destroyed, with all our costumes burned, we had lost even greater wealth. We were essentially penniless, and we had no way to rebuild. We certainly could not compete in the cath without all the tools of our trade.

We were doomed.

And yet Taggart insisted he was planning something. He sat inside his wagon all day long, his windows shuttered against the dust of the road. At every meal Goran brought him scraps of food—a bowl of porridge, a round of Keon's quickbread.

When Goran returned from the wagon, he always reported that Taggart was doing nothing. The old man had parchment spread before him on his table and a pot of fresh ink neatly capped by his side. But each day, every breakfast and supper, the parchment remained blank. Taggart merely stared at the far wagon wall, smoothing his beard over his iron necklace. He seemed oblivious to the fact that we were completing our journey, that we were drawing close to Lutecia.

Goran disappeared after each time he served Taggart. He always returned to camp with filthy fingers. At first he tried to hide his actions from me, but soon enough he let me watch him feed treats to Wart—worms, or crickets, or other bugs he had been lucky enough to catch. I was no judge of wriggling beasties, but Wart seemed content with the offerings. Certainly, the toad must be grateful that she didn't need to hop into potential danger, seeking out her own food.

One night, after Goran took Wart off to bed, I spoke to Caw by the campfire. "What do you think Goran and Wart say to each other?"

*"I have no idea."* Caw ruffled his feathers, as if I'd insulted him by asking.

"But you're a darkbeast!"

*"I'm your darkbeast."*

The response warmed me more than the flames by my side.

Still, I pushed. "Can't you hear what other darkbeasts say? Don't you know what Goran and Wart say to each other, mind to mind?"

Caw made the low, rumbling sound that told me he was disappointed in me, that I had failed to learn one of his lessons. *"Certainly, I can speak to Wart. All of us darkbeasts share a common tongue. But when Bestius ties together darkbeast and child, he makes the bonds unique. It's not a matter of hearing, of seeing. It's a matter of being."*

I nodded, feeling the resonance of Caw's last word in my very bones. I could not imagine any meaningful words passing between Goran and Wart, certainly not as much as the conversations I had with Caw. Nevertheless, the toad appeared to offer Goran some small comfort in the midst of all we had lost. I was happy he had that much.

I first viewed Lutecia one week before the Hunter's Moon. Nothing had prepared me for the sight—not the stories I had heard as a child, not the whispers and rumors as we drew near. The Silver River ran far slower here than it did near my home village; its banks were so far apart I could not throw a stone from one side to the other. As the sun slipped below the horizon, we rounded a wide bend in the road.

I caught my breath when I saw the plain spread out before me.

The Silver River broke into a dozen strands, and each of those fractured into a dozen more. Like an infinite mosaic, the river unspooled before us, stretching a hundred watery fingers into the sea.

And there was Lutecia, sprawling across those liquid veins. The Primate's city was beautiful. Snow-white walls soared to the heavens, punctuated by a score of red-capped towers. I could make out half a dozen gates from my current vantage point, each seeming more secure than the last, each boasting wider strips of iron, each sheltered behind a broader swath of water. In the distance the sea glinted at the city's back, announcing safety and security to all.

"The Primate's Pearl," Goran said. I'd never heard the name before, but I understood it instantly. Lutecia was as beautiful and shimmering and hard and impenetrable as any precious stone. "We'll have to hurry if we're going to make Nuntia's Gate by moonrise."

"Nuntia's Gate?" I surprised myself by discovering I still had a voice, even as I was lost in amazement at the city spread out before me.

"Each of Lutecia's twelve gates opens to a different class of visitor. Soldiers enter by Marius, merchants by Aurelius. We Travelers bear messages in our revels, new lessons for the primacy. Nuntia lets us enter."

The drivers were already urging the horses forward. I soon realized, though, that there were few direct paths across the plain. Some roads that looked clear turned out to be dead ends; paving stones simply gave way to vicious, sucking mud. Other paths looked hopeless, but they led to bridges, to solid arches of wood or stone, to safety and security. Even with our expert drivers, we needed to backtrack twice, to find bridges sturdy enough to bear our Traveler wagons. It was all part of the Primate's defense, Goran explained to me. All part of keeping Lutecia safe.

We arrived at Nuntia's Gate just as a sliver of moon crested the horizon. As we creaked to a stop on a narrow islet, a beleaguered official wandered out of the postern door. He bore a long scroll in one hand and a ridiculous white plume in the other. His velvet cap hung askew on his head, the rich fabric marked with inky fingerprints where he obviously had the habit of nudging it higher on his skull. "Name?" he called out as he approached. A lifetime of fatigue coated the single word.

"Taggart."

"Taggart," repeated the official greeter. "Taggart. Taggart." He rolled the name around his tongue another dozen times, tilting his scroll this way and that, as if he sought a better angle for reading in the dim light. I wondered what would happen if we were not on his list. Would we be permitted to spend the night here, at the base of the city walls? Or would we be required to cross back over the watery plain, to thread our way among bridges and footpaths, hoping not to slip into some unseen channel?

"Ah, yes," the official said at last. He scratched his nib across the parchment page. "Taggart. You'll lodge in the second bay of the Garden of Madrina. Welcome to the cath. May Nuntia watch over all your efforts and guide you in the ways of the Twelve." The man dug deep in his robes and produced a sheaf of parchment sheets, each embossed with a crimson ribbon. He fumbled through them with his ink-stained fingers. Finally locating the one meant for us, he passed the document to Goran with a hurried bow.

The words sounded like a formula, and I suspected Goran was supposed to offer up some fine, flowery response. Instead he clutched the beribboned page and trotted back between the wagons, making sure that every driver had the vital information—second bay, Garden of Madrina.

Nuntia's Gate was narrower than the one we had used in Cooper Falls. In fact, our largest wagons passed through with only an arm's length to spare on either side. The gate was long, though. The city walls were thick, two rods at least. When we emerged, we found ourselves in a shallow courtyard. I was surprised to find yet another gate before us, guarded as well as the first, equipped with an identical portcullis. I looked up and caught my breath.

Soldiers stood on the wall above us, their uniforms announcing them as the Primate's Guard. Each man held a longbow, with a sturdy quiver strapped across his back. Every third soldier had an arrow nocked to his string. The warning was clear. If any of us Travelers took a step in the wrong direction, if any of us charged the inner gate, we could all be cut down in a heartbeat. I wondered what other weapons the men held, how many other ways I could die.

While we were stranded in the courtyard, another official checked Taggart's name against a list, confirming that we were indeed destined for the second bay of the Garden of Madrina. We waited an eternity as the inner gate creaked open—all the time, the Guard kept their arrows trained upon us. I did not draw a full breath until we had passed out of the courtyard.

Once, I had thought that Silver Hollow held the limits of my world. When I traveled to Rivermeet, I imagined I had seen everything a city could offer. When I arrived in Cooper Falls, I came to comprehend the error of my ways, the flaw in my understanding.

But none of those places had prepared me for a city the size of Lutecia. None of them had made me understand the power and the glory that was the stronghold of Primate Hendor.

We passed godhouses large enough to hold every man, woman, and child in Silver Hollow, with space to spare for sheep and dogs. Lutecia's streets merged together in vast squares, forming lakes of stone that could easily drown the familiar grassy green I had crossed every day of my childhood. Broad fingers of the Silver River flowed through the city, carving the land into islands, into broad spits. Intricate bridges arched above the water, some standing higher than half a dozen men, their careful stonework picked out by oil lamps that glinted against the night sky.

Everywhere I turned, there was another wondrous sight. Buildings so tall they leaned against each other across a narrow street.

A round counter in a stony square, built around a well-tended fire where a fat woman sold sausages to every man, woman, and child who passed her a gleaming copper coin. Three godhouses in a row, each dedicated to Tempestia, all linked by chutes of water that threw plumes of spray into the night sky.

There were checkpoints throughout the city, narrow passages where soldiers ordered us to display our papers. Each time, Goran produced our parchment page, complete with its crimson seal. Each time, he announced that we were Taggart's troupe, that we were present for the cath. Each time, we were passed into a different quadrant of the astonishing tangle of stone and water and sky that was Lutecia.

By the time we arrived at the Garden of Madrina, my eyes felt numb from viewing so many amazing things. We settled in our generous corner, in the second bay. Even as we set up camp, I could not help but feel like an impostor. We had no revel. No stage. No costumes. We had come all this distance, but we had nothing to offer Primate Hendor, nothing to secure five years of tax-free travel through Duodecia.

I stared up at the statue of Madrina in the center of the garden. She was tall and dark and mysterious in the night. Perhaps if we found her godhouse in the morning . . . Perhaps if we offered up our greatest dedication, our promises to worship her for all the years to come . . . Maybe then she might help us.

No one else would.

And every other troupe in Lutecia would be sending up similar prayers. Every other troupe would plead for religious patronage. There was nothing special about us. Nothing that would help us to succeed.

Lost in morose thought, I had forgotten about Caw. My darkbeast reclaimed my attention, though, when he flew to the top of the Madrina statue, settling on the goddess's head.

"Caw!" I exclaimed. "Get down from there!"

*"I can see the entire garden from here. I can tell you about all the other troupes. Do you want to hear?"*

Before I could think of a threat terrible enough to get my darkbeast to return, Taggart's wagon door opened. I had not seen him for days. His face had grown thinner as we traveled north. His beard seemed lighter in the moonlight, as if it were spun of silver. Once again I was struck by the ornate decoration of his iron necklace; it seemed as if the metal itself writhed beneath the moonlight.

"Come," Taggart said. Even though he did not raise his voice, everyone in the troupe heard him. His words gathered us in, as if he had spread an iron net around us. Even Caw left his vantage point on Madrina's statue, rocketing down to perch on the top of Taggart's wagon.

"Gather close," our leader said. "It is time for me to tell you of our revel, and how we'll win the cath."

# Chapter Eighteen

*T*he *Darkbeast*," Taggart said, and it took me a moment to realize he was speaking the name of a revel. His eyes seemed hollow; they caught the moonlight and splintered it back with a crazy glow. His fingers spread wide as he raised his right hand, as he pointed toward Caw atop his wagon. "We'll weave our revel around a darkbeast."

*"What a fine idea!"* Caw cackled inside my thoughts.

The troupe exploded. They had tried a new revel, and they had failed. They had never worked a revel around a darkbeast before. They had no time to learn a new revel, to build a new show. They couldn't, they wouldn't, they didn't know how.

Taggart waited until the last whisper of protest melted into the night. Only when every last Traveler was silent did he deign to speak again. "I understand what you're thinking. I know you are afraid. But this revel will be different from *The Twelve*. Allow me to explain." His gnarled hands raked the air, urging everyone to step closer.

Obviously intrigued, Caw flew down to settle on my padded shoulder. He cocked his head, the better to hear Taggart's words. I held my breath, as if that would let me concentrate better, see everything more clearly.

Taggart nodded slowly before he extended his right index finger into the air. He looked for all the world like Patrius, instructing the gods in the ways of the world they ruled. "First," he said. "We frightened people with *The Twelve* because it was a Holy Play. Villagers did not understand how we meant to meld the traditional pieces, how we meant to bring new words for the gods. We've learned our lesson. We will not be so bold again. *The Darkbeast* is a Common Play. No god will be shown."

Several of the Travelers murmured their understanding.

"Second," Taggart continued, warming to his counting. "We have few resources. We need to work a revel that is simple—no stage, no costumes, no face paint. But we can turn that necessity to our favor. All the other troupes hope to impress the Primate with their riches, with their glory. Our revel will stand out for its very simplicity. Its purity."

More murmurs from the Travelers. They knew their craft well. They understood the need to stand out. In a world where all wore diamonds and silks, common wool could attract the eye.

"Third," Taggart pronounced. "We must offer up atonement to the Inquisitors. Messenger birds have certainly reached Lutecia, well in advance of our own humble wagons. We are being offered a gift here, an opportunity to atone, or we would never have been permitted past the gate of Nuntia. But every Inquisitor in Duodecia knows our story. Every Inquisitor will watch for the slightest flaw in our revel, the tiniest misstep. Therefore, everything we do must be with an eye toward abasing ourselves. Toward offering up our wrongs. In the most literal of ways, we must take our failings to our darkbeasts."

Silence. Every one of the Travelers remembered offering up faults. Each remembered a darkbeast taking on those human weaknesses. They all recalled the moment of release, the lightness, the perfect joy of darkbeast magic. But no one could imagine what Taggart meant now, how he intended to fold our personal flaws into a public revel.

"Goran!" Taggart said. "When is your nameday?"

"The night of the Hunter's Moon," Goran answered immediately.

Taggart nodded. Of course he had already known his own grandson's answer. "Primate Hendor's nameday as well. The night of the cath." He waited for each and every Traveler to nod, to acknowledge the truth behind his words. And when the troupe was watching with undivided attention, he said, "Picture this! A bare stage. Two Travelers step into the center, a young woman and a boy. One has recently dispatched her darkbeast, has taken on the mantle of responsibility, of obligation. The other is ready to leave behind his failings. To become a man."

Half of the Travelers stared at Vala, half at Goran. Me, I turned toward Caw, my eyes almost crossing as I brought him into focus. When Taggart spoke, I felt his words deep inside my bones, as if I'd known them forever.

"Each Traveler will join the circle of witnesses, reciting the name of his own darkbeast. Remember—the trick is in the details. We convince our audience to believe our general stories by telling them specific truths."

I thought back to the first night I had spoken with Taggart, the night when Goran had caught me on the steps of the Travelers' wagon. Taggart had quizzed me about the Twelve's sigils then. He had penalized me for overlooking the telling details, the most specific truths.

Taggart spun out the last of his new revel. "Our newest adult, Vala, will invoke the protection of Bestius. She will accept the child's nameday gift. She will kindle the incense and confirm that he has a valid tax tattoo. And then, before the community of all worshippers, beneath the watchful eye of the Inquisitors who are certain to gather for our revel, before all the priests and priestesses and the Primate himself, Goran will slay his darkbeast." He held up one twisted hand to stop the troupe's startled reaction. Taggart's voice was strong and steady as he proclaimed, "Our revel will end with the next child stepping forward, silently offering up her perfect faith and dedication. With her very presence she will vow to follow in the footsteps of Goran, of Vala, of all the other loyal adults. Keara will close the revel by displaying Caw, by offering him up for imminent sacrifice."

The troupe exploded, even as Caw darted to the top of the nearest wagon.

*"I won't do it, Caw!"* I thrust the thought into his mind with more force than I had ever used before. I would not slay my darkbeast, ever. I had not done so for Mother, for my family, for Silver Hollow and the life I had led for twelve years. I certainly would not do so for Taggart, for the Travelers, for the cath.

But Taggart had not said I must slay Caw. He had only said I must stand before the audience. I must offer up the *imminent* sacrifice. Show a glimpse of the future.

Around me, some of the Travelers thought Taggart's plan was magnificent, a public display of humility, of submission. Others thought the revel was certain to be a disaster, another challenge to people who were afraid to think of anything new, to witness faith in unfamiliar terms. Goran stood off to the side, his face washed pale in the moonlight. He swallowed hard, his jaw set with some unspoken determination.

I closed my eyes and tried to imagine being surrounded by the Travelers, by the audience, by the Primate's court itself. I pictured myself with Caw on my shoulder, his feathers glinting in torch-light. I saw myself delivering Taggart's lines, some perfectly balanced couplet that pledged my devotion to the Twelve, to Bestius, to the long history of darkbeasts slain year after year after year.

Would the gods strike me down, then and there? Would they destroy me for daring to lie in such a public way? My belly twisted, and I thought I would be ill right there, in the second bay of the Garden of Madrina, in front of the troupe I had thought to call my family.

But I could not gainsay Taggart. Not now. Not when the entire future of the Travelers depended on this revel. The Travelers had carried me away from Silver Hollow, and so they were my family, now and forever.

*"It will not be real,"* Caw said, as if he had arrived at the same conclusion I had, following the same road to a common destination.

*"Never,"* I vowed silently. *"We would leave them and be alone till the end of our days before I would ever make it real."* I thought I heard Caw's heartbeat echoing through my mind.

And so we all agreed. Taggart had pleaded his case well. Every one of the Travelers understood our desperate straits; no one could truly argue for any other revel, for any traditional play to win the cath. We slept that night in full concord, united in our understanding that we must perfect *The Darkbeast*.

I thought I had seen the Travelers work hard before. I thought they had pushed themselves to learn lines, to sew costumes, to weave the magic of a revel.

That was nothing compared to the work they put into *The Darkbeast*.

Morning, noon, and night, a half dozen members of the troupe worked on lines, developing the finest rhymes for Vala, the perfect couplets for Goran. *The Darkbeast*, of course, was a Common Play. No god would be depicted on the stage. We could not be accused of sacrilege, of crafting a new Holy Play. Nevertheless, our revel needed to be special. It needed to be shocking. It needed to be perfect.

That perfection started with the costumes. *The Twelve* had failed, in part, because no one had ever seen robes like the gray ones before—uniform representations for the great variety of the gods. This time the troupe needed to look familiar. Common. As comforting as possible. The revel would be performed for the Primate himself, and for the judging priests and priestesses, but we Travelers must look like the very essence of commoners, like every loyal subject within the borders of the primacy.

Once again I found myself in demand as an expert on village life. I offered advice on the proper length of an apron. I expressed my opinion about the amount of dirt that should be rubbed into a wool-clad elbow. I thought hard about scuffed shoes, comparing the marks on heels and toes. I tried to picture every villager I had ever known, every man and woman and child who had ever killed a darkbeast in a sheltered village godhouse of Bestius.

The greatest challenge involved Wart herself. No one could train a toad. No one could teach her how to swell her throat, how to flick her tongue at the precise dramatic instant.

Instead we needed to emphasize her cage, to draw the audience's eyes away from the details of that particular darkbeast. We needed to make each person in the audience remember the feel of his own leash, recall his own dark thoughts, the ones that he had offered up for the first twelve years of his life. We needed to bring to life our staged version of Bestius's godhouse, the darkened building represented by our empty stage.

That last bit proved the greatest challenge for me. Three separate times I started to comment on the moment of slaying Goran's darkbeast. I caught myself before I said, "When *I* saw the priest . . ." I swallowed the words, "The children sounded so far away when *I* was inside the godhouse. . . ." I barely remembered not to admit, "The thing *I* remember most is how hungry I was, how much I wanted a bite of seedcake. . . ."

Whatever else happened, whatever else I shared, I could not let anyone know I had entered Bestius's godhouse with Caw on my own twelfth nameday. I could never divulge that I had spared my darkbeast.

For seven days the troupe labored. For one chaotic week we shaped our revel. We tested ourselves, smoothing our work into utter, flawless perfection. And finally we rehearsed our revel the final time. From start to finish we performed as if the Primate himself were present, as if all the priests and priestesses were arrayed before us. We hit every mark. We delivered every line.

Vala was not perfect; she was still a weak version of her former self, stumbling over lines, missing precise marks. Nevertheless, she threw all she had into her cold demand that Goran take on the mantle of adult responsibility. Goran charmed us all, honoring the darkbeast who had served him well, even as he plotted her demise. I found the perfect note of bravery as I walked to the front of the stage at the very end of the revel, wordless, grave. I folded my fingers into a fist and held my hand above my head, waiting for Caw to settle himself in absolute stasis. We made the perfect tableau, an image that would be burned into the audience's eyes forever.

The moon was high above the Garden of Madrina when we finished that last rehearsal. The sky was completely clear; not even a wisp of cloud ghosted across the stars. I suspected there would be a film of ice on the city wells by dawn.

My breath fogged before me as I strolled away from the other Travelers. I needed some time to myself, some space from the constant pressure of others. As I sank onto a stone bench in a distant corner of the garden, I realized I had not been alone since arriving in Lutecia.

Caw consented to my holding him against my body. I worried he would catch a chill in this darkest hour of the night. I felt an overwhelming gratitude that he was with me, that he was alive and well in the midst of our repeated depiction of darkbeast death.

"By this time tomorrow," I whispered, "we'll know if we've won the cath." The thought amazed me. We had traveled so far, worked so long in hope of such a victory.

*"All for the price of a darkbeast."* Caw's voice was as bitter as the mudroyal that had bound him to me years before.

Truth be told, I feared that price. I did not want to watch Goran perform on a stage what every child was supposed to do in the secrecy of Bestius's godhouse. I was terrified of the moment when he plunged his knife into Wart's squat body.

But even if Goran were not committed to killing Wart on stage, he would have executed her in Bestius's godhouse before the full moon set. That was the way of darkbeasts; it had been done since the first Primate sat upon his throne.

I kept my voice low. "What, Caw? What would you have me

do? I told you I will never make the revel true for us. I will not kill you."

*"How long do you think we can stay here, Keara? If the revel fails, how long will the Travelers tolerate an outsider like you? How long will they protect and feed a stranger, in the face of their defeat?"*

"The revel will not fail!" I fought the urge to shout. I was not sure if I was trying to convince Caw or myself. "Why are you always so negative?"

*"That was not negative."* He shifted his body, pulling away from my chest enough to ruffle his feathers in his familiar show of disdain. With a vehemence I'd never heard from him before, he thought, *"This is negative: What if the revel succeeds? What if the Travelers win the cath? How long before they need to repeat the revel in front of another audience? How many children are in the troupe, Keara? How many are close to slaying their darkbeasts?"*

*Vala had been,* I thought. *And Goran.* All of the other Traveler children were in Austeria. No one else was even old enough to cry the show.

I understood the question behind Caw's words, the bitter truth he set before me like a poisoned banquet. "What would you have me do, Caw? It's a lot more complicated than when I spared you on my nameday!"

I expected Caw to contradict me. I expected him to explain that we *could* walk out of the Primate's fine city and find another path, discover another road. I expected him to say we could be safe and independent, that all would be right.

But Caw said none of those things. Instead he flapped his wings in an ungainly way, pushing off from my chest to land in an awkward huddle by my feet. Before I could lean down to pick him up, he pointed his beak over my shoulder and thought, *"Vala!"*

I turned around to see my former friend glaring at Caw and me. The moonlight picked out the wild tumble of her hair. The stars etched the pools of her eyes, outlined the firm set of her lips. I thought I was snared inside a nightmare as she said, "What have we here, Keara-ti? But that's not right, is it? No person past her twelfth nameday should ever be called '-ti'! What evil are you plotting with your darkbeast, heretic?"

Before I could respond, before I could explain, she turned on her heel and disappeared into the night.

# Chapter Nineteen

I did not sleep that night.

After Vala left, it took a long time for me to find the courage to return to the Travelers' camp in the second bay. I did not speak to anyone in the troupe. I did not laugh or rant or cry as I waited for my former friend to reveal my secret. I knew she must disclose that I was a girl who had not killed her darkbeast.

Part of me believed I should just take Caw and flee. But another part of me believed my best chance for safety was to stay with the troupe, to act as if everything was fine. I could lie to them, lie to everyone. I could say Vala had misunderstood what she had heard. She had misconstrued some innocent tale

I told Caw. I could even accuse Vala of making up the entire conversation, of crafting false words to spite me.

I was not thinking clearly; I was desperate for any means of escaping my fate.

I still had not chosen a course of action by dawn. As the troupe awoke, all the other Travelers ignored me. They were lost within their own worlds, worrying about lines, fretting about costumes. A tremendous energy roiled through our camp. For the first time in weeks, the Travelers had true hope, real confidence that they might actually win the cath. I tried not to disrupt that excitement by revealing my own terror of Vala.

Shortly after sunrise Taggart returned from a meeting with the leaders of all the other troupes. Together they had drawn lots to determine the order of our revels. For days the Travelers had debated which slot was best. Some said the first, because that made the deepest impression on the audience. Some said the last, to leave a final vision before the judges. Everyone agreed the midafternoon times were the worst.

The Twelve had smiled upon us. We had drawn the last time.

As a group we traveled to the theater, making our way past half a dozen checkpoints in the city streets. Caw came with us, of course—we needed him for the revel's dramatic conclusion. I let him set his own pace, flying ahead of me or lagging behind.

Every time I got a glimpse of his midnight plumage, I swallowed down the acid bite of fear.

I clutched my cloak close around my shoulders and drew up my hood, as if that flimsy fabric could shield me from Vala's wrath. As much as I disagreed with her, as much as I knew that she was wrong, that she misunderstood me, I had to admit I could comprehend her furious reaction.

Vala had welcomed Slither's death, even though it meant giving up the momentary joy of darkbeast magic. She had been willing—eager—to lose one thing in order to gain something she valued more, her expected place in Traveler society. But after sacrificing Slither, Vala had lost her strength on stage. She had lost the absolute conviction of her words. It might take her weeks, months, years to find a new balance, the new power of being a woman.

Vala had played by the rules, and she had lost.

And I had cheated. Vala was never going to let me get away with my crime. With my sin. The only question was when she would take action.

At last we arrived at the theater. Taggart chivied us through a giant arch, pushing and prodding until we had climbed a hundred steps. Other Travelers climbed with us; other troupes headed to their places at the top of the magnificent theater.

From that aerie we could look down on the stage where we would perform that night. The other Travelers were familiar with the sight; they had played the cath before. I was astonished, though, by the scene before my eyes.

The amphitheater was cut into the very bedrock of Lutecia, carved into the single largest expanse of stone that hulked between the endless channels of the Silver River. Rocky benches marched toward the stage; already the seats were filled with thousands of eager citizens. The stage itself was a marble platform worn smooth over the centuries. A towering wall stretched behind it, taller than any ten men, looming like a mountain, specifically designed to throw Travelers' voices back over the audience, amplifying the slightest sound.

Giant niches were cut into the wall, thirteen in all. Each held an image of a god or goddess, three times the height of any living man. In the very center stood a statue of the Primate himself. The Twelve all wore painted garments, complete with lifelike sigils. But the carved Hendor was dressed in cloth of gold, finished with a golden crown.

A pavilion was erected at the front of the audience, covering half a dozen rows of stone seating. The Primate's seal was woven into the great swaths of crimson silk. The enclosure was surrounded by an entire company of the Primate's Guard—twenty of the famed armed men. I could make out their obvious weapons— swords, crossbows, short blades at their waists. I tried not to think about the other tools they carried, their secret ways to kill a man or woman, to execute a child.

As I gaped at the guards, a line of priests and priestesses made their way to the enclosure. I knew without asking that they were going to judge the cath—those twelve religious figures, along with the Primate, who must already be ensconced upon his throne. Each wore the attire specified for one of the Twelve—long black robes for Bestius, shimmering rainbow scarves for Nuntia, a sturdy linen kirtle for Madrina.

The finery was almost enough to make me forget Vala, to make me overlook my danger. Almost, but not quite.

I took care to sit on the end of a rock bench, huddling next to Goran in hopes that no one would think twice about me. I tried to take some comfort in Wart's iron cage near my feet. Perhaps the pending death of one darkbeast would atone for the salvation of another.

It wasn't like Goran actually loved Wart. It wasn't like he longed for her company, the way I had Caw's. Goran was a good boy. He would be a good man. And his transition from child to adult, his execution of Wart, would give the Travelers all they needed to win the competition.

I made Caw hide beneath my cloak, tangled in the impossible hope that Vala would stay silent if she did not see my darkbeast.

When the revels finally began, I was so overwhelmed with the power and majesty of the other Traveler troupes that I almost forgot my fear.

The first company offered up *Pondera and the Broken Scales*. They had clearly poured their energies into creating their costumes. Pondera's silks were the most luxurious I could imagine. The woman who played the goddess had applied careful paint around her eyes. Across the great distance I could not be certain, but I thought even her eyelashes were gilded.

The man who played the merchant, though, seemed overwhelmed by the watching crowd. He forgot his lines. Three times he needed to be prompted by one of his companions. Applause was tepid by the time the performers finally left the stage.

*"Not bad,"* Caw said. *"If the audience is willing to wait for a line or three."*

*"Their costumes were gorgeous."* I thought my response. After the night before, I felt as if it would never be safe to speak aloud to Caw again.

*"Not from my perspective."* He shifted, and I knew he was demanding to be released from the darkness beneath my cloak. I eased a hand beneath the wool and stroked him from the crown of his head to his tail, in a way I knew he loved. Nevertheless, I was not going to bring him out. I was not going to chance inflaming Vala's anger.

Instead I looked at our troupe, gauging their reaction to the revel. Many of the adults were engaged in a spirited discussion of what had made *Broken Scales* good, of what the performance had lacked.

Uncharacteristically, Goran did not join in. Instead he muttered to himself like a madman. Only when I leaned close did I realize he was rehearsing his lines.

As I stared, he dug a scrap of folded wool out of his pocket. I was astonished to see him pluck three wriggling grubs from the cloth. He offered them, one by one, to Wart. Each time the toad took one of the treats, Goran ran his fingers over every bar of the cage.

In the pause between revels I had to look for Vala, had to see what she was thinking. It took me only a moment to find her condemning gaze. She sat amid a clutch of other women. They all seemed to be discussing the performance we had just watched, but Vala was eerily silent. She stared at me, her black eyes unblinking. I barely resisted the urge to reach again for Caw's smooth feathers beneath my cloak, to soothe myself by tracing their familiar ridges.

The next revel began with little fanfare. It was *Tempestia and the Sheaf of Wheat*, one that we had considered and discarded because we had feared that the words might remind Primate Hendor of his inauspicious past. The revel told of a magnificent city on a hidden plain in the center of Duodecia, where Tempestia's weather-working spun wildly out of control. Whirlwinds mixed with thunderstorms; sunshine beat down through torrents of rain.

These Travelers knew the words of their piece. Their voices were pleasant, and they were loud enough to be heard in the very back row of the giant theater. Their version of Tempestia's weather, though, looked as if they wanted to protect frightened children. The whirlwind was nothing more than a single piece of gray silk spun in a circle by four excited boys. Thunder was made by pounding on a pair of slack-skinned drums. Lightning was mere sunlight concentrated by a half dozen mirrors. As the company took their bows, some people in the crowd jeered.

Caw shifted against me. *"Now, that was a fine revel."*

*"No,"* I thought. *"It wasn't."*

*"But they knew every word! And they were loud enough to hear, too."*

*"Volume isn't everything,"* I remonstrated. *"In fact, volume is almost nothing at all."* As if haunted by my own words, I had to seek out Vala once again.

She was standing this time, leaning against the arch that led to the winding staircase. She crossed her arms over her chest, erecting a rigid barrier to conversation with anyone. A breeze caught her hair, churning it into a dark cloud. The entire time I stared at her, her eyes did not stray from mine.

The third company staged *Mortana and the Dance of Death.* The work was a grim one, about the goddess of death's brutal destruction of a godhouse built by a faithless village. The performers had gambled—and lost—on drawing one of the later time slots. The words of the revel clearly stated that the action took place at night, under a wicked moon, beneath cold, uncaring stars. A complicated costume change assumed the actors could shelter unseen as the woman playing Mortana transformed from a common milkmaid into a wrathful goddess. As the sun beat down from a cloudless sky, the revel seemed unbearably warped. Even the horror of death meted out by an angry immortal seemed laughable. The revel's words were completely mismatched with its action.

After the performance I explained to Caw what had happened. *"Perhaps they should have performed under a giant cloak,"* he said helpfully. *"Trust me. That would have been dark enough for any costume change."*

Despite myself, I started to laugh at Caw's aggrieved tone. I could ill afford to be so glib, though. I steeled myself to look for Vala, to meet her open condemnation.

But this time my former friend was nowhere to be found. She no longer lurked in the archway. She had not returned to her seat with the women. A part of me argued that she could have gone to use the privy. She might be rehearsing her lines. Perhaps she had grown hungry, and she had left the theater for a sausage or a bite of bread.

But another part of me was certain that Vala had made her decision. She had chosen to destroy me. She had elected to denounce Caw, the darkbeast who should have been long dead.

I considered fleeing the theater. But where would I go? How far would I get without the parchment pass that had vouchsafed our troupe every step of the way through regulated

Lutecia? Which bridges could I follow to escape my fate?

*"We're safe enough here, in the theater,"* Caw said from beneath my cloak.

*"You haven't seen her. You don't understand how angry she is."*

*"I haven't seen* anything." Caw's complaint was as pointed as the claws he dug into my thigh.

*"Take my word for it. It is not safe."*

*"You should know by now—nothing is ever perfectly safe. Nothing is ever secure."*

Caw's calm pronouncement echoed in my thoughts. Nothing . . . There was nothing I could do. Nothing I could say. Nothing I could change, nothing I *would* change, to turn back the months since I had spared my darkbeast in Bestius's godhouse. I had made my choice on my nameday, and all the intervening weeks, all the nights slept under the changing moons, all the leagues I had covered with the Travelers, could never make a difference.

Why condemn my darkbeast to the shadows beneath my cloak if I could not guarantee his safety? I sighed and flung back the edge of the garment. Caw wasted no time hopping free from my lap. He tilted his head as he settled on my shoulder and nodded toward the stage. *"Another revel begins. This one I intend to watch."*

And so it went for the rest of the afternoon. One company had brilliant staging. Another chose the perfect revel to perform, lyrical words that praised the Primate's peace, that predicted prosperity for all the years of his realm. A third troupe had the best voices I had yet heard on stage.

But I had become enough of a Traveler that I could see how every performance was flawed. Every show was broken in some way—sometimes minor, sometimes so extreme that I caught my fellow Travelers whispering, wondering how anyone dared to bring such an offering before Primate Hendor and the gathered judges. How had they ever thought to win the cath?

Through it all I watched and waited, and I worried about Vala. I was helpless to do anything. My fate—and Caw's—rested entirely in her hands.

# Chapter Twenty

At last it was time for us to wind our way down the hundred stairs. Taggart led the way. I wiped my sweating palms against my sides, moving my shoulders enough that Caw ruffled his feathers in annoyance. *"Stop it,"* he said. *"If you're that afraid, then let us just leave. We can duck into that alcove there."*

I shook my head. The alcove was a bare indentation in the theater wall, suitable only for a very skinny statue. I sighed gustily, making Caw fight for yet another new position. *"Fine, then,"* he said in exasperation. *"Go back up the stairs. Take another seat in the theater and watch the Travelers perform."*

"You're not helping!" I thought, wiping a slick hand across my forehead.

*"There! Go through that arch. We can take our chances in Lutecia."*

*"Stop it, Caw. I've thought of all those things and more. But we'll never escape—not if Vala has truly left the theater to summon Inquisitors. Not if she intends to enlist the help of the Primate's Guard."*

*"Fine,"* Caw said, settling more firmly onto my shoulder. *"As long as we're done with that foolishness. All will be well, Keara-ti. You must have faith in all the Twelve."*

Faith in all the Twelve. That would be a lot easier if I hadn't broken their rules. If I hadn't defied Bestius by keeping Caw alive.

And this wasn't just about the Twelve. It was also about the Travelers. They were counting on me; I had a role to perform.

For the first time in my life I was going to stand on a stage in front of an audience. I had no spoken lines, but my presence was the crucial conclusion to our revel. The promise of another child executing another darkbeast—of *all* children executing *all* darkbeasts—that was the most important note of our play. That was the image to win the cath.

And maybe, just maybe, my role would redeem me. Even if Vala denounced me in front of the Primate himself, in front of all those priests and priestesses, my presence in the revel might bring some forgiveness.

Or so I argued to myself, over and over, as Taggart guided us through the tangle of passages behind the stage. I was soon utterly confused by the turns, by the short flights of stairs, up, then down, then up again. I suspected we had passed far beneath the stage itself when we finally stopped in a small, dim room.

Our trunks were stacked against the wall. The Travelers lost no time donning their simple costumes. They did not need to fuss with face paint. There were no awkward wigs, no heavy items to lug onto the stage.

Caw flew to a corner while I donned my own midnight robe. I tugged my hair free from the collar and twisted my neck, making sure the garment hung straight.

"Goran!" Taggart boomed, and I was not the only Traveler who jumped. "Stand here. Put that cage on the ground. Do not move. Not a step."

Goran complied, but a frown creased his brow, an unusual show of temper. I realized he had not eaten for the entire day, like any penitent child entering Bestius's godhouse. For that matter, neither had I. Neither had most of the Travelers; we had all been too busy watching our competition.

Taggart ordered the chorus of adults to take their places behind Goran. Each was dressed in the common attire of a villager. Each was prepared to give witness to a long-ago-slain darkbeast, to the failings confessed over the course of an entire childhood. Each was made anonymous by the very details of our revel.

Finally, Taggart ordered me to stand at the end of the line. I would wait behind the grown men and women, my presence hidden by my dark robe. Only after Caw was situated on my shoulder did Taggart call for Vala, demanding that she take her place beside Goran. "I don't have time for this foolishness," he muttered after a moment. "Vala! Stand forward!"

Nothing.

I should say something. I should tell Taggart that Vala had left during the afternoon, that she had fled the theater while the other troupes were performing. There was no time for me to explain, though. There wasn't a chance to tell about Caw, about the godhouse in Silver Hollow, about the Inquisitors who sought me even now.

"Where is she?" Taggart bellowed. I worried that his voice was loud enough to reach the stage. He would be heard by the Primate, by the priests and priestesses, by the entire city gathered in the theater.

I needed to explain. I needed to tell the truth. And yet my despair blocked my throat, kept the words from coming. I could not have confessed if my life depended on it, if Caw's life did.

A rumble of applause reached us, vibrating through the ceiling, through the walls of our close little room. The revel before ours had finished. It was time to take the stage.

"We'll change the revel," Taggart said grimly. "*I* will speak Vala's lines."

*"I don't think that is a very good idea,"* Caw said.

*"Hush!"* I dared not rebuke my darkbeast out loud.

Taggart knew every word of the play, of course. He had listened to Vala recite her rhymes every day for the past week. Without a doubt, the presence of an old man instead of a young woman would shade the meaning of the revel, would twist the vision for the Primate and priests and priestesses, for all who watched.

But what option did we have?

Taggart glared at all of us. I thought he narrowed his eyes specially when he gazed at Caw. "Enough gaping!" he said at last. "The cath must be ours!"

And then he led us through the snarl of corridors to the stage. We were silent as we walked. Any hint of hope, of confidence, had been washed away by Vala's absence. We had no chance of winning the cath. Everything would be lost. Without money, without costumes, without face paints or sigils, we were doomed.

*"I think—,"* Caw started to say, and his tone was calm, reassuring. Nevertheless, I cut him off.

*"No, Caw. Not now. I can't listen to you now."*

When we emerged onto the stage, I had to blink hard. The sun had set while we were underground. Torches now flared on either side of the marble platform. A delicate system of oil lamps had been kindled across the front of the stage—each clay lantern burned with a golden flame that was reflected back onto the stage by polished silver mirrors. The effect was dazzling—it was bright enough to hide the stars in the sky above us. It was almost bright enough to block the moon.

As we huddled in the arched doorway, Taggart walked to the center of the stage. He ignored the lights completely, making the deepest bow I had ever seen. With his ancient head still touched to his knee, he proclaimed, "Your Majesty! Priests and priestesses of all the Twelve! Citizens of fair Lutecia! We humble Travelers offer up these new words, written solely for this cath. We call our play . . . *The Darkbeast.*"

Excitement rippled through the crowd. Of course no other troupe had dared to launch a new revel during this cath. No other company had even tried an existing Common Play. Murmurs of speculation buoyed us as we moved to our marks—a gentle arc that spread behind Taggart and Goran. I lurked behind the center position, my head as deep inside my hood as an Inquisitor's, my hands folded into fists so that my fingers did not reflect any light.

Caw sat on my shoulder. He knew to keep his wings furled and his eyes turned away from the audience, away from the prying glint of oil lamps.

Once we all stood ready, Taggart spread his arms wide, letting his cloak shimmer in the golden light. The gesture hid Goran behind him, keeping the audience from forming even the slightest suspicion about our revel, about the magic we intended to work. Taggart's great beard shifted over his familiar necklace, and the tangle of iron seemed to amplify his voice as he boomed his opening lines:

> *"Namedays come and namedays go, and old men*
>    *barely know*
> *The names of boys, the names of girls, whose dark-*
>    *beasts' blood must flow."*

Astonished, I realized what Taggart was doing. He was composing rhymes as he stood there. He was improvising new lines, wiping away the recitation Vala would have made. Her words had been crafted for a young woman, for a new adult who had slain her darkbeast only a few short weeks before. Taggart spoke with the wisdom of age, with the burden of a long life.

We Travelers were reckless for considering a new revel at the cath.

We were positively mad to compose one on the spot.

Goran, though, acted as if he had spent the past seven days rehearsing with Taggart on the stage before him. Weighing the moment perfectly, he ducked beneath his grandfather's outstretched arms, placing himself squarely in front of the reflecting oil lamps. The audience started to whisper among themselves, trying to figure out this new game before them, trying to parse the unfamiliar lines, the unexpected appearance of an unmasked, unpainted boy.

Goran raised Wart's iron cage. The motion revealed the single extravagance in our production—the elaborate leash that bound him to his darkbeast. Our entire company had argued, long and hard, about that bond. On the one hand, we intended to look as much like common village folk as possible. We wanted our revel to re-create the vast world beyond the Primate's court, to bring alive the experience of every citizen of Duodecia, even the most lowly swineherd.

On the other hand, we needed to illustrate the power darkbeasts held over our lives. We had to demonstrate how we were bound to the creatures, how they guided us, how they tethered us to a course of right, and good, and justice.

After days of debate we had agreed to pour our most creative energy into Goran's leash. Cloth of gold was woven between lengths of silk, all the colors of the rainbow folded in upon each other. Tiny mirrors traced the seams of the cloth. Deeply cut glass jewels lined the edges. The leash glimmered as if it were the Primate's most precious possession; the finery stood out all the more for being the only point of color on an unadorned stage of black and white.

Goran held his hand at the perfect angle, stretching the leash to best display its beauty. When he finally responded to Taggart's introductory phrases, he kept his voice light, young. If there could be any doubt in the audience's mind, Goran began with the most important fact: "This night I mark my nameday, full twelve years I've lived. . . ."

The audience grasped the significance immediately. Even from my vantage point behind the adults, I felt the crowd's interest flare. They caught their breath. They leaned forward on their benches. After a long day of familiar revels they were finally being treated to something new. Something no one had predicted.

Taggart responded to Goran's recitation, making up new rhymes. He extolled the virtues of the darkbeast bond, of being tied to a creature that was tasked with taking on our worst secrets, our most vile thoughts.

Goran took care to display leash and cage and poor drab Wart, as if he'd been born for the role.

One by one the other players stepped forward. Each named a long-ago-slain darkbeast. Each recited a catalog of failings. Each intoned, "I gave it to my darkbeast. She took it. It was hers."

He took it. It was his.

She took it.

He took it.

Over and over and over.

"*Why make such a spectacle out of this?*" Caw asked grumpily. "*That's what we are meant to do.*"

"*Hush!*" I thought.

*"I'm just saying, a darkbeast would be worse than useless if it couldn't handle a few minor failings."*

*"Caw!"* My voice was sharp inside my own skull. *"This is the most important part of the revel!"*

And it was.

Each of the Travelers now stood perfectly still. Their faces were turned to the unseen moon. Their postures contained a faint reminder, a dying echo of darkbeast magic. Each seemed lost in the memory of that floating feeling, that never-forgotten sensation of utter, unmatchable lightness. The Travelers spread their fingers, connoting the tingle, the hum, the thrumming sensation of giving up a fault forever.

The adults were arranged in three short lines, effectively making a box that cut Taggart and Goran off from the rest of the world. Their bodies formed walls, like the walls of Bestius's square godhouse. Only the view of the audience was left unobstructed.

Taggart stepped to the very front of the stage. He raised his arms, and his voice echoed all the way to the back wall of the theater.

*"All Lutecia is a godhouse, and Bestius's priests look on,*
*The Primate brings the Twelve here, to watch this*
*    darkbeast pawn*
*Meet his death—long waited; meet his death—now*
*    proud.*

*This boy does what he must do, for you, the*
*watching crowd."*

The audience started to hum as Taggart tossed a handful of incense onto a small brazier in the center of the godhouse square. Goran silently offered up a gift, a single gilded apple that glinted in the light of the oil lamps. Taggart reached for Goran's wrist, checked for a valid tax tattoo, nodded in satisfaction.

Taggart glided to the back of the stage. Goran stood in the square, with only a caged darkbeast toad between him and the crowd.

Carefully he placed Wart's cage upon the floor, taking care to center the iron between two mirrored lamps. With a flip of his wrist he tore free of his elaborate jeweled leash, sending the embellished fabric in a soaring arc before it pooled upon the stage. He pulled an iron blade from his belt, a simple two-edged knife, and he held it high in his right hand. Then he turned it from side to side, guaranteeing that everyone in the audience could make out what he held.

That was my cue to prepare for my entrance. I extended my hand for Caw to settle in place. Goran would slay Wart, and then the line of adults would part. I would step forward, taking my place at the center of the stage, before Primate Hendor, before all of Lutecia. I would raise the knife sheathed at my waist, hold it high as a hint of the next darkbeast death to come.

My heart pounded so loudly I could never have heard a word from Caw.

I could still see Goran's face in profile. His jaw was set. Droplets of sweat stood out on his upper lip. His eyes were wide, and he blinked too quickly.

This was the moment. This was the thing that would make our revel different from all the others. We were about to show a rite that was always kept secret; we were about to reveal the instant that was sacred to Bestius.

Goran was supposed to kneel before Wart's cage. He was supposed to slide open the iron door. He was supposed to grasp his darkbeast in his left hand, raise the knife in his right.

But he did not move.

*"Maybe we shouldn't kill our darkbeasts."* Goran had said the blasphemous words after Vala performed so poorly in *The Twelve*. Now his voice echoed in my memory, a whispered explanation of why he was frozen. *"Maybe we shouldn't kill our darkbeasts."*

I caught my breath. Goran needed to reach into the cage. He needed to execute Wart. He needed to kill his darkbeast so that I could step forward, so that we could end the revel and win the cath. Anything else, any further delay, and all the priests in the theater would declare him Lost. They would summon Inquisitors, take Goran prisoner, treat him far more harshly than he had been treated in Patrius's godhouse, months ago, back in Rivermeet.

Taggart must say something. I must present Caw. We all must act to preserve the illusion that we had woven for the Primate, for the priests and priestesses, for all the people of Lutecia.

"Halt!"

The word rang out, a thousand times louder for ending such a long gap of silence. I recognized the voice, even as my heart lurched in my chest.

Vala. Vala had returned to the revel. I squinted, forcing my eyes to focus past the oil lamps. Vala had come back—and she had brought an entire company of Inquisitors. They flowed down the side aisle of the theater like a white tide, ready to swamp the Primate's pavilion. Ready to drown all of us on stage.

The Travelers before me broke rank, drawing back, falling to either side in scrambling horror. "Halt!" Vala cried again. She was pointing to the stage, past Goran, past Taggart, past the entire troupe, to me. "Stop that one! The girl with the raven! The girl who failed to kill her darkbeast!"

The audience boiled over like porridge in a forgotten pot. Women screamed. Men bellowed. The Primate's Guard shouted out orders as they closed ranks, protecting Primate Hendor from an evil they could barely identify.

The Inquisitors ignored all of that, though. They focused on only one thing—me. I felt their eyes burning beneath their pure white hoods. I imagined the freezing fire of their hidden knives.

My throat closed at the thought of their chains slashing tight around my flesh.

I told my feet to move. I told my lungs to breathe. I told my body to save me, to take me away from certain torture and death, for me, for Caw. And yet I was transfixed by the disaster that flooded the theater.

"Now, girl!" Taggart bellowed, and his hands bit into my shoulders. He had shoved Goran in front of him, snagged me with the same gesture. The other Travelers were scattered around us, aimless, panicked.

Caw squawked and took to the air, finally freeing me to move.

Taggart wasted no time on further instructions. Instead he pounded past our astonished fellow Travelers. He led the way into the tunnels behind the stage. I had no chance to look back at the Primate, at the priests and priestesses who sat in judgment, at Vala, at the dozens of Inquisitors who hollered for my blood.

I followed Taggart, running for my life.

# Chapter Twenty-One

We ran. We ran like I had never run before. We ran like I had never *imagined* running before.

Through the tunnels behind the stage. Into the labyrinth of stone passages on the outskirts of the theater. Into the streets of Lutecia. Over bridges. Beneath arches. Through the Garden of Madrina, the Garden of Marius, the Garden of Venerius.

Thrice we were stopped by guards and asked for our papers. The first time, Taggart drew himself to his full height, catching his breath with the astonishing control of a man born to the Travelers. He imperiously presented our parchment with absolute confidence that no warning could yet have reached the checkpoint. Our passage was still—for the shortest of times—safe.

The second time, we pushed past the guards, startling men who expected no real challenge, who were lulled by the fact that almost all of the city's residents were caught up in the thrill of the cath back at the amphitheater. The third time, Caw swooped out of the dark night sky, flying directly into the face of the captain who demanded that we stop.

But after evading the furious guards that last time, we needed to walk. Taggart, for one, could not keep up the pace he had set; he pressed his hand against his side as we strode rapidly through the city streets. Goran followed, apparently stunned into silence as he cradled Wart's cage against his chest. I matched my pace to theirs, trying to ignore the panic itching between my shoulder blades, the burning pressure to *run, run, run!*

Caw settled on my padded shoulder, digging in his talons fiercely. *"Caw . . . ,"* I said, uncertain of what I was going to tell him. I was terrified to be chased by Inquisitors and the Primate's Guard. I was overjoyed that Goran had saved his darkbeast. I was confused that Taggart was leading us deeper and deeper into Lutecia's darkest streets.

*"Save your thoughts,"* my darkbeast said. *"You'll need all your concentration."*

As always, Caw was right.

Before, I had thought Lutecia was a wonderland of shimmering stone and running water. Now I discovered that the oldest buildings were made of wood—rotten, stinking planks mired in pools of slimy water. The gutters were filled with disgusting lumps of decay—the cloudy eyes of dead fish, the contents of countless chamber pots, reeking masses of flea-infested hay. I did my best to breathe through my mouth, and I gathered up the edges of my cloak, trying to keep its hem from the worst of the filth.

We passed through a tangle of streets, heading into narrower lanes. Those paved paths gave way to muddy alleys, to passages so narrow that Taggart's shoulders scraped against the wooden buildings as we scuttled forward. He hunched lower, curving his spine until he seemed no taller than Goran.

From that vantage point he paused before a narrow wooden door. The planks were scarred, as if they'd been kicked by count-less filthy boots. Taggart's fist landed in the center of the boards, and he pounded out a quick tattoo—two rapid taps, followed by one, followed by three more. I held my breath—partly out of anxi-ety, partly out of a desperate desire to keep from inhaling any more of the alley's stench.

Taggart was raising his fist to pound again, when the door swung open. The woman on the threshold was tiny; my chin could have rested atop her head. She wore a scarf over her snow-white hair, and her face was carved with valleys as deep as the Silver Riv-er's canals in the city behind us. Her left hand curled into a tight claw, the muscles rigid as stone where they jutted from beneath her sleeve. She took in Caw, huddled on my shoulder, and Wart, clutched tight in Goran's grip. As she gestured for us to enter, her right arm trembled, a rhythmic palsy that made me want to stare.

There was no time to gape, though. No time to do anything but duck inside. Goran stumbled closer to the fire, holding out his iron cage as if Wart were cold, as if the toad needed comfort after the chaos of our flight. Caw brushed against the crown of my head as he flew to perch on the worm-eaten fireplace mantel at the far side of the room.

The space was nearly bare. There was a pallet in one corner, close enough to the smoky fire that I wondered if I would dare to sleep there. A rough table stood by the door, flanked by a pair of stools that looked like they might collapse in a stiff wind. A giant spiderweb filled the corner above the makeshift bed, and my belly turned as I made out the shape of a fat spider lurking in the center, its body the size of my fist.

"Brigid," Taggart said. "We need to flee."

"What will you be needing?" The woman's reedy voice matched her hovel. Her breath whistled as she spoke, and I realized she was missing nearly all her teeth.

"A skiff. Food, if you can get it. Water or wine."

The old woman nodded, saving her breath for the effort to throw a moth-eaten cloak around her shoulders. By the time she was ready to open the door again, Taggart had dug deep within his robes. A silver coin glinted between his finger and his thumb. "Be careful," he said. "The Inquisitors are involved."

Her ragged snort indicated she did not fear any white robes. Nevertheless, she tugged her scarf lower over her brow, as if to disguise herself before she ventured out. She barely paused on the threshold, raking over Goran and me with surprisingly clear eyes before she ducked away.

"I'm sorry," Goran said as soon as the door closed. His whisper was so soft I barely heard him. He spoke to Taggart and to me, but he stared at Wart, at her dry, bumpy skin, at her bulging, round eyes. "I couldn't . . ." His throat seemed to close around the rest of his words.

Caw shifted, but he remained uncharacteristically silent inside my head. That very silence, though, made a pressure rise in my chest. "It was me," I said, and my vehemence seemed to warm the walls around us. "Vala summoned the Inquisitors because of me." I held up my tattooed wrist. "She found out my nameday was back at the Thunder Moon. I should have killed Caw then."

I waited for their condemnation, for their well-deserved outrage that I had brought disaster upon the Travelers. I waited for Taggart to shout at me, to decry all I had done and—far more important—not done. I waited to be told I was a liar and a cheat, that I must take my chances alone in the streets of Lutecia. I waited for Caw alone to compliment me, to tell me I had done well by finally telling the truth, to say I was a good girl and a brave one.

But Goran only stared into the fire, his fingers ever restless on Wart's dark cage. And Taggart ignored my confession. Instead he fiddled with his iron necklace, with the intricate metalwork that seemed to reinforce his power and his stature, even now that he was separate from all the other Travelers. And Caw remained silent.

"I'm sorry," I said, unconsciously echoing Goran. "I should have told you both earlier. I never should have stayed with the troupe."

Taggart slipped his iron ornament over his head, looping the heavy iron strands between his fingers. Once his shoulders were free, he shrugged, as if he had shed a weight far greater than that of the carefully worked design. He stretched his hands toward the smoking flames, clenching his fingers into fists around the necklace's strands, releasing them, clenching them again.

Unbidden tears heated my eyes. Taggart wasn't going to say anything—not to Goran, who had risked everything to save Wart. Not to me, who had placed our lives in danger even earlier.

I fought against my old feelings of despair. It seemed that nothing I did would ever turn right. I could never return to Bestius's godhouse to do the thing I should have done, way back upon my nameday. I could not change time. More important, I did not *want* to change it. Even now. Even when I feared that Inquisitors would burst through the door at any moment.

Despite everything, despite my hunger and my thirst and the unbounded pool of exhaustion that made my muscles twitch, I would never slay Caw.

I swallowed hard and tried to push down the sobs rising in my throat. I blinked in an unsuccessful attempt to banish my tears. I stared into the fire, hoping to steady myself, to weave together the last shreds of my composure.

Out of the corner of my eye I saw it then. An impossible ripple. A shudder of iron where metal should not move.

I squeezed my eyes shut for ten heartbeats, telling myself I was imagining things. But when I looked again, when I stared directly at Taggart's heavy necklace, I found that my eyes had not deceived me.

The metal *was* moving.

No. Not the metal. The slender black lizard that wove between the iron whorls.

Its tail lashed from side to side. Its head turned to a sharp angle. Its tongue flashed toward me, withdrew, flashed again.

Taggart's low voice rumbled. "Well then. You have both apologized, and it is time for me to say that I am sorry as well." He turned to Goran. "I'm sorry to have crafted *The Darkbeast*, now that I see how you truly feel about Wart. If I had known, if I had understood, I would have found another way."

Goran barely nodded, his mouth slack as he stared at the night-black lizard.

Taggart waved a veiny hand, taking in both of us as he said, "It is time you met Flick. He's been watching you for long enough." I could only stare as the darkbeast scrambled up Taggart's arm, then down his robe and up the wall to the mantel, where he came to rest beside Caw.

*"I suppose that lizard for supper would be a very bad idea?"*

I was too stunned to respond to Caw's wry question. Goran seemed as amazed as I. His hands trembled as he steadied himself against the wall, easing his weight to his knees. He settled Wart's cage on the ground harshly enough that the toad hopped into a new position. "You?" he croaked at Taggart, even as he stared at the shimmering black lizard.

"Me. And Brigid." He waved a ropy hand toward the massive spider in the corner of the room. "And Keara, of course. And now you."

*"Well, isn't this a party?"* Caw said. *"And fresh spider is off the menu as well."*

I had to trust my voice. I asked Taggart, "How long have you known, about Caw and me?"

"Since the night Goran caught you outside my wagon."

"How?"

"People were eager for your nameday, back in Silver Hollow. They looked forward to the feast. The very first night we played your village, I saw your hunger to come with us. I waited for you, you know. Why else would a troupe of Travelers spend six nights in a tiny village in the middle of Duodecia?"

I had no answer. I could barely remember those six nights. They seemed like a lifetime ago.

Taggart said, "When you finally showed up in our camp with your darkbeast at your side, I knew you had not completed the nameday ritual."

I swallowed hard. All those days, weeks, months, Taggart had known. . . . When the Inquisitor stopped me in Rivermeet and Taggart sent Goran to Patrius's godhouse in my place . . . Here, in Lutecia, with Vala restless for revenge . . .

Goran's hands settled on his hips. A touch of his old swagger returned as he asked, "And you? You've had . . . Flick all this time? You spared your darkbeast too?"

Taggart nodded solemnly. "There are a handful of us who don't believe the Twelve ever intended us to slay our closest companions."

"But the Inquisitors—," I began.

"We hide from them as best we can. We seek out people like ourselves when we are able. We help the handful who would be wholly free, who would remain true to themselves and to their first soul-matched companions. Their darkbeasts."

Remain true. I thought back to Silver Hollow, to the long nights before my nameday, when Mother had leashed me to Caw's cage. Offer up my rebellion, she had ordered, and I had tried. I had brought those negative thoughts to my darkbeast, and he had taken them, over and over and over again.

But I still had my rebellion. I had kept it alive, burning past my nameday, past the time I was supposed to slay my closest friend in all the world.

I had offered up my fear as well, when I was a young girl, when I had worried about the silliness of ghosts. Yet fear had dogged me as I fled Silver Hollow; it had driven me to hide from the Inquisitor on the Great Road. It had led me to the Travelers' camp, to Taggart.

Back in Silver Hollow I had offered up my jealousy when I believed that a dance and a village boy were the most important things in my life. Caw had agreed to take that jealousy, to spare me from those thoughts. Nevertheless, I had been jealous of Vala, of her success with the troupe, of the role she had claimed ahead of me.

And I had offered up despair, the fruitless belief that my world was crumpled amid soggy lacemallow and a raging fever and a rainstorm I thought would never end. Despair had trailed me, though, driving me to the cath, hounding me through the streets of Lutecia.

Rebellion, fear, jealousy, despair—and a thousand other dark emotions I had offered up to Caw over the years. He had taken every one of them, told me to forget them. And yet they remained mine. They remained *me*.

*"I wondered how long it would take you to realize that,"* Caw said.

*"You knew all along?"* I thought to him. *"That I held on to my bad thoughts? That I continued to be evil?"*

*"You're not evil. You're human."*

Human. Like Mother—she could be prideful, impatient, short of temper. But she had surely offered those failings to her darkbeast when she was a child. If the priests were right, those faults should have been taken from her years before.

Caw bobbed his head, as if he approved of the direction of my thoughts. I tried to reduce my confusion to words. *"What good is a darkbeast, then? If we're left with all our faults even after we offer them up?"*

Caw hunched his shoulders in the closest move he could make to a shrug. *"You identify your failings and I take them. My action makes you more aware of your fault than you were before. After that, you try to avoid doing wrong. You aren't perfect—no one is—but you're better than you would have been. Because you believe in me, you come to believe in yourself."*

That made sense.

The system worked because everyone *believed* that it worked.

Everyone—Mother, my sisters, all of the adults in Duodecia—*believed* in the power of darkbeasts, without asking more questions. And because they believed, the system continued, year after year, child after child, darkbeast after slaughtered darkbeast.

But why was it necessary to kill our darkbeasts? If speaking to the creatures was enough to make us better people, then why kill them just as we became adults?

Caw shifted from foot to foot. *"People kill their darkbeasts because tradition says they should. Following rules makes them feel safe, feel that they belong. They even give up the thrill of darkbeast magic for the greater good."*

But that was not all, I realized. People killed their darkbeasts because the priests told them to. Priests who accepted nameday gifts in honor of the ritual. Priests who gained power and prestige and control over all the people. Priests who could back up their rules with the might of Inquisitors.

Caw cocked his head to one side. *"There is that, too. It takes a rebel to fight against the Twelve."*

*"Not the Twelve,"* I thought. *"Against humans who claim to speak for the Twelve. Ordinary people who have twisted the ways of the gods."*

Ordinary people. Like the Inquisitor who had come to our camp in Rivermeet, intent on collecting his bribe to keep our revel secret. Like the Primate's Guard who had ranged about the stage at the cath earlier that very night. Like the guards who had tried to stop us as Taggart helped us to flee the amphitheater, to escape certain torture at the hands of the Inquisitors.

I glanced at Taggart now. He was holding out his hand so that Flick could twine around his wrist. I realized I had fallen silent for far too long. I owed the old Traveler a response to the truth he had shared.

"So," I said. "Where can I find these others? What do I do now?"

"No," Goran replied before Taggart could. "What do *we* do now?"

"*We*," Caw repeated with a sarcastic lilt. *"Wonderful. If it's 'we,' then the lizard and the spider are definitely off-limits. I will need a treat or two, you know. To sustain myself in the face of all this change."*

I dug deep in my pocket and found a pellet of dried bread for my darkbeast. Then I settled by the fire and waited for Taggart to explain what we were going to do. How we were going to live. What life was going to be like in a world where people spared their darkbeasts.

# Epilogue

It's been a week, and we're still hiding in the marshes north of Lutecia.

Brigid helped Taggart, Goran, and me more than we ever dreamed—she got us a wherry and a sack of food and three flasks of water. She handed over a dozen silver coins as well; I often stay awake at night trying to figure out how she got them. What they cost her.

On our first full day in the marsh Goran exchanged clothes with me. He went back to Lutecia as a girl. He couldn't get in the city gates, of course, not without a pass. But he managed to buy goods from the merchants who were waiting to enter. He got us three good blankets and an iron pot.

We're lucky we all had knives—Goran and I from the revel, and Taggart always keeps a blade about him. The old man is always prepared. Has been ever since he was a child.

Taggart showed us how to bind reeds into bundles, how to fashion them into a shelter that is dry, and warm enough if the three of us huddle together at night. Goran has made us fishing poles, and I can always find plants that are good to eat. So far we haven't gone hungry, even if Caw insists he never has enough to eat.

Taggart says there are other darkers out here, people who have spared their darkbeasts. We'll have to travel away from Lutecia to find them, though. The Inquisitors have too strong a hold here, with all of the godhouses, with the Primate himself.

We're just waiting for the Autumn Meet to end, in one more week. We'll travel the Great Road south with other people then. We'll hide from the Inquisitors with the crowds returning to their own villages.

And somewhere we'll slip away from the throng. We'll find the other darkers.

And Taggart says that when we do, it will be time to make some changes. It will be time to make our presence known, all of us. Everyone who has been brave enough to move beyond tradition.

It is time to stand up to the Inquisitors. It is time to demand our place in the world, with our darkbeasts by our side.

Caw and Flick agree, but Wart isn't sure. She's not used to thinking for herself. This has been such a change for her; she always expected Goran to execute her, just as he was supposed to do.

Every day I think about Vala. I think about the way she shared her blanket with me. I think about toffee bread melting across my tongue. I think about how Vala was my first true friend.

I've never hated anyone before. I've never felt the fire of that emotion, the certainty, the blind insistence. I've always believed it takes too much emotion to remember all the wrongs, all the reasons to despise another person.

I don't hate Vala now.

But I'm fairly certain she hates me. Me, and Goran, and Taggart. And Caw. Wart. Flick, if she knew that the lizard existed.

It will be a long winter. We'll walk a hard road. But Caw insists it will be worth it in the end.

*"Forget your worries,"* he tells me every night as I'm about to fall asleep. *"I take them. They are mine."* And I feel my body grow as light as the clouds that scuttle across the moon. My fingers tingle, and my breath hums in my throat, and I know I have made the right choice, no matter what dangers we'll face when the sun rises on another day.

Continue Keara and Caw's journey in

# Darkbeast
## REBELLION

So very, very cold. I stumbled forward, suddenly freed from a pine tree's clinging fingers. For one terrible moment I thought I was going to fall again, was going to jam my knee another time.

Goran's fingers closed around my arm. He held me upright, gripped me tightly until I caught my breath. "Must rest," I whispered, surprised to find that my lips were chapped, raw, and swollen from the wind.

"No," he said.

I shook my head. "Jus' a second." The words slurred, frozen as they left my mouth.

"We can't stop, Keara." Goran looked exasperated. Exhausted. And something else. Something I could not read. Something I should understand. Something . . . And then it came to me. Goran was afraid.

I took another step and slipped on the ice that had frozen in Taggart's footsteps. I sat down hard in the snow. I was too weary to cry out. I started to shiver, great racking waves that shook me from my chin to my toes.

"Keara," Goran pleaded. "Stand up. I know you can. Come on."

I shook my head. The motion freed my jaw enough that my teeth began to chatter.

Goran knelt beside me, gritting his own teeth in frustration. I watched through slitted eyes as he fumbled in his pocket. I could see his fingers close around something, and I watched indecision swirl across his face.

What? What was he holding?

Goran caught his breath and drew his hand from his pocket. Despite my fatigue, despite the bitter cold that shook my body, despite the clatter of my teeth in my aching jaws, I craned my neck to see what he held.

It was a bracelet. A fine black bracelet, spun out of delicate fibers. Careful, ornate knots marked the circumference at regular intervals.

"Wha' is it?" I asked. My curiosity was piqued, even if I found it even harder to form words.

"It belonged to my mother," Goran said. I understood the importance of that simple statement. Goran *never* spoke about his mother. His mother. Taggart's daughter. "She gave it to me when she . . . left."

Left? Where had she gone? I peered closer at the treasure. I had a dozen questions I wanted to ask.

Goran seemed to understand the most important one. "It's

from her darkbeast, a ferret. She spun the fur after she killed Streak. Tied the knots to make it stay on her wrist. To remember the lessons she took to her darkbeast."

I'd seen such things before. My mother had stuffed her rat darkbeast and kept him by our hearth. My sister had turned her snake into a belt. But this bracelet was finer than those tributes. It was beautiful. Precious.

"It's yours," Goran said. "But you have to get up, Keara." He dangled it in front of me.

I shook my head. He asked too much.

"Keara. I'll give it to you. But you must walk."

I heard the tears in his voice. The desperation. The terror.

And I looked at the darkbeast bracelet again. He had never shown it to me before. It must be precious to him, perhaps the most valuable thing he owned. I caught my tongue between my teeth. I flexed my toes within my soaked boots. I caught my breath. And I stood.

Goran nodded, taking a few steps down the path. Jerkily, I followed. One step. Two. Three.

Goran slipped the bracelet around my blue-veined wrist, covering the tax tattoo that showed I was a loyal citizen of Duodecia. He tightened the knots carefully, cinching the jewelry so that I could not lose it in the snow.

And we continued down the forest trail.

I could not say how long we stumbled. I could not say how many times I fell. I could not say how many hours we trudged through the snow. But finally, when I thought I would never take another step—precious darkbeast bracelet or no precious darkbeast bracelet—I caught myself against the edge of a gigantic black stone.

Dazed, I looked around. We stood in the middle of a clearing. I had grown up in the woods near Silver Hollow; I knew my way around a forest. I immediately realized that something was different about this space.

The line of trees behind me had been groomed. Nothing obvious, nothing that any casual traveler would notice. But the more I stared, the more I could see that the clearing had been shaped into a definite square.

The black stone only drove home what my mind had already started to accept. It wasn't perfectly smooth beneath its cap of snow. There were indentations on the two sides visible to me, and I could see a groove in the top, along one long edge.

The clearing was shaped to resemble a godhouse, a building sacred to Bestius. I tilted my head back to gaze at the lowering sky, almost as if I were a toddler trying to catch snowflakes on my tongue. The clouds loomed over the forest, closing in the space, making the clearing feel even more like the holy home of the god of darkbeasts.

A shiver quaked down my spine.

I had not been in Bestius's godhouse since the Thunder Moon. I had not been in the presence of the god of darkbeasts since I had been instructed to take Caw from his iron cage, ordered to wring his neck and take my place among the adults of Silver Hollow.

My raven chose that moment to alight on my shoulder, startling me so badly that a wordless cry burst from my lips. *"Hush,"* he said. *"All will be well. They might even have a few treats to share."*

"Th-they?" I stammered, fighting the urge to turn my back on the black stone and Taggart and Goran, to push my way back into the safety of the forest.

Before Caw could answer, though, before I could flee, the meaning of his words became clear. Two dozen shadows detached themselves from the trees. Two dozen dark figures glided toward the altar in the center of the clearing. Two dozen people surrounded Taggart and Goran and me.

I opened my mouth to scream, but no sound came out.

Fortunately, Goran was not as tongue-tied as I. "What do you think you're doing?" he shouted at the hooded figures. Angry as he was, he kept his left hand deep in his pocket. I was certain his fingers were curled around Wart, keeping his darkbeast warm. Gaining some comfort from the toad's lumpy skin.

Caw's talons tightened around my shoulder—not enough to draw blood through the padding, but enough to command my attention. He cocked his head toward the stone, toward the altar. I understood what he was saying. I should move forward, get the rock at my back. I should take a stand beside Goran and Taggart.

Except Taggart was not standing beside the altar.

Instead the old man had stepped back toward the edge of the

trees, closer to our attackers, closer to the slippery, frozen path we had created reaching this cursed place. As I gaped, the old man reached inside his cloak, his fingers diving deep beneath his tunic. I was shocked to see him pull out Flick, to display his living dark-beast to everyone. "Well met, good friends," he croaked.

"Well met, indeed."

The voice belonged to a woman. She stepped forward from the shadows, simultaneously raising her hands to push back the hood of her felted wool cloak. Her fingernails flashed and her hair glinted in the light of the Frost Moon. The icy blond strands sparkled, nearly as bright as the snow.

She stared hard at Taggart for several heartbeats. Still silent, she glanced at Goran, and then her gaze settled on me. In the moonlight it looked as if her eyes were clear, as if her irises held no color at all. Her pupils were very wide, and I somehow felt as if I might fall through them into another world, a place as dark as the altar at my back, a place where there was no Frost Moon, no snow. Only endless, velvet night.

"Keara," she said, and her voice thrummed with power. Those strange eyes narrowed, and she shifted her gaze just the slightest, to take in the raven on my shoulder. "Caw," she said, the word dropping down to a whisper.

I longed to reach for my darkbeast, to find comfort by strok-ing his feathers. I dared not move, though. Not with the woman staring at me. Not with her knowing our names, knowing so much more than I. I concentrated on the bracelet Goran had given me, trying to draw comfort from its knotted strands, even as I feared to say or do anything.

It was Goran who broke the spell. "My lady," he said, collapsing into the deepest bow the Travelers used on stage. "You have us at an advantage. You ken more than we do."

I recognized the rhythmic line from one of the revels, one of the Travelers' plays that Goran had memorized from the first day he could talk. A quick glance at Taggart confirmed my suspicion; his cracked lips twitched into a painful smile. Even exhausted, even freezing and ill, he was proud of his grandson. Proud, and apparently relieved that we all were safe.

In for a sapling, in for the woods. I'd cast my lot with Taggart and Goran when we fled the Primate's city. I'd be a fool not to trust them now, the first time we were seriously challenged on the road. On the road, or *off* it, to be more precise.

The woman looked gravely at Goran, never suggesting that she was even faintly amused by his Traveler airs. "I am Saeran," she said. "I am the leader of these folk."

Goran seemed to gain courage from her gracious reply. "These folk, then? Who are they?"

Saeran's brow was smooth in the moonlight. She seemed utterly unaware of the bitter cold, completely oblivious to the snow that spread beneath her narrow boots. "We are the ones you seek. We are the Darkers."

Darkers. At last. Just as Taggart had promised—wary people who kept their secrets in the wilds of Duodecia. They held on to their darkbeasts, child and adult alike. They defied the Primate and Inquisitors. They banded together, traitors and heretics all, to fight the injustice of the Twelve.

As if to prove her words, Saeran shifted her weight, extending her left arm in front of her body. A ray of whiskers appeared from her sleeve, followed by a frantically twitching, jet-black nose. The darkbeast edged into the moonlight, its tiny claws gripping Saeran's arm. A rat. Only when the creature had emerged fully from the woman's sleeve did it curl its long, naked tail around its body, hunching its shoulders as if it felt the midnight chill. Or as if it were afraid.

"This is Twitch," Saeran said.

I heard a lifetime of conflict in that pronouncement. Saeran said her darkbeast's name with honor and respect. But there was something harder underneath her tone—something that sounded like teeth gritting together in a nightmare.

Caw heard it too. He shifted his weight on my shoulder with the ease of long practice. I could feel his chest move close to my ear. I imagined I could hear his heart beating, fast and wild beneath the stars. *"What?"* I asked. *"What is wrong here?"*

*"Perhaps nothing."* Caw tilted his head to one side, as if he were trying to peer into the rat's mind.

*"Can you talk to him? Can you hear Twitch?"*

*"Yes. No."*

*"What does that mean?"*

Caw made a chittering sound at the back of his throat. It wasn't the noise he made when he was afraid, though. Rather, it told me that he was curious, that he was nearly lost in thought. *"I can hear the rat think,"* he said at last. *"And I can feel its bond to the woman. But that bond is . . . different from yours and mine."*

*"Different? How?"*

*"I cannot say, precisely. I can sense mudroyal—the taste is strong in the ties between them."*

My tongue curled in reflex. Mudroyal was one of the most bitter herbs Mother had stocked in our cottage. *"And ladysilk? Is it there too?"*

Mudroyal and ladysilk were the herbs used by Bestius's priests in the bonding ceremony that linked a newborn child to a dark-beast. The herbs somehow enhanced the god's magic, cementing the ties between human and animal.

*"Aye,"* Caw said, bobbing his head. *"There's ladysilk, too. That much is like any other bonding."*

I might have asked Caw more questions. I might have struggled to learn more about what worried him, what felt different. But by then Saeran was speaking again. "You must be tired," she proclaimed. "Fear makes the road stretch long."

I wanted to argue that I wasn't afraid. But I had only lived with the Travelers for a few months before the disaster in Lutecia, and I had not yet mastered the confident tone that came so easily to those who spent a lifetime performing on a stage. I could not make my lie believable, not to one with a gaze as shrewd as Saeran's. I stayed silent and let Taggart answer for all of us.

"We would be grateful," he wheezed, "if you would conduct us to your darkhold."

The relentless battle between good and evil—
the Light and the Dark—has raged since the
beginning of time. But suddenly, evil surges and
threatens to claim absolute victory. Can the Light
overcome, or will all good be destroyed forever?

"A tale of mounting
excitement, suffused with
legendary, mystical, and
allegorical overtones."
—*Horn Book*

Newbery Honor Book
*Boston Globe*—
*Horn Book* Award
ALA Notable
Children's Book

"Breathtakingly
impressive."
—*Kirkus Reviews*
IRA/CBC Children's
Choice

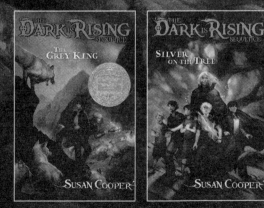

Newbery Medal
*Horn Book* Fanfare List
ALA Notable
Children's Book

★"Not to be missed."
—*SLJ*, starred review

PRINT AND EBOOK EDITIONS AVAILABLE
From Margaret K. McElderry Books ★ KIDS.SimonandSchuster.com